RAIDER

'You knew,' Flora hissed at him. *'You knew what was happening to Laurie on board the Arctic Raider, didn't you?'*

There was a mystery about the boy's death, about the drowning forty years ago on a deep-sea trawler. What really happened? What was the truth about the 'Iceman', the sinister captain of the ship? Why didn't he go back and look for the boy who'd fallen overboard? Who is telling the truth about that fateful Christmas on board the *Arctic Raider*?

This is what Flora and Maddy have to find out.

Susan Gates was born in Lincolnshire. She has a degree in English and American Literature from Warwick University. She's worked in secondary schools in England and in Africa. She now lives in County Durham and has three children

Other titles by Susan Gates:

White Stranger
ISBN 0 19 271830 4

Trish longs to be like Grace, already a woman, black and confident. But Grace treats her like a child and ignores her. Then Grace asks Trish to visit her home, and it seems as if she'll become 'best friends' with Grace at last. But there are painful discoveries in store for Trish . . .

Humanzee
ISBN 0 19 275038 0

Nemo has seen some sights in his circus life, but nothing like Chingwe the humanzee in the Wonderland freak show. One look at the creature—part human, part chimpanzee—sends Nemo into a rage. You can't put people in cages!

Iron Heads
ISBN 0 19 271755 3

'This book is both exciting and thought-provoking.'
Books for Keeps

Firebug
ISBN 0 19 271735 9

'Surreal events balanced by psyc⟨...⟩ redoubtable story of pyromania a t⟨...⟩

RAIDER

Other Oxford Fiction

Chartbreak
Gillian Cross

The Hounds of the Morrigan
Pat O'Shea

The House of Rats
Stephen Elboz

Against the Day
Michael Cronin

It's My Life
Michael Harrison

Chandra
Frances Mary Hendry

Sweet Clarinet
James Riordan

Witchy
Ann Phillips

RAIDER

Susan Gates

OXFORD
UNIVERSITY PRESS

OXFORD
UNIVERSITY PRESS

Great Clarendon Street, Oxford OX2 6DP

Oxford University Press is a department of the University of Oxford.
It furthers the University's objective of excellence in research, scholarship,
and education by publishing worldwide in

Oxford New York

Athens Auckland Bangkok Bogotá Buenos Aires Calcutta
Cape Town Chennai Dar es Salaam Delhi Florence Hong Kong Istanbul
Karachi Kuala Lumpur Madrid Melbourne Mexico City Mumbai
Nairobi Paris São Paulo Singapore Taipei Tokyo Toronto Warsaw

and associated companies in Berlin Ibadan

Oxford is a registered trade mark of Oxford University Press
in the UK and in certain other countries

First published 1995
Reprinted 1996, 1997
First published in this paperback edition 2000

British Library Cataloguing in Publication Data available

ISBN 0 19 275059 3

1 3 5 7 9 10 8 6 4 2

Typeset by AFS Image Setters Ltd, Glasgow
Printed in Great Britain by Cox & Wyman Ltd, Reading, Berks

20 December 1952
Off the coast of Iceland

'Get out of the way!' screamed the mate of the *Arctic Raider* at Laurie. 'Get out of the way, you useless little sod! You'll get your head took off!'

Laurie, 16 years old, couldn't feel his feet. They'd frozen to the deck and he was blinded by ice particles driving in from glaciers.

The other skippers in the fleet had long ago run for shelter. But not the Iceman, skipper of the *Arctic Raider* and a legend in his own time. He was still fishing.

Laurie could see nothing. The jelly in his eyeballs seemed frozen solid. His eyelashes were crystals. The wind sliced through his oilskin as if it were tissue paper.

'Where's them needles?'

That was Laurie's job. To fill the big wooden needles to mend the trawl nets. It was all he was fit for. After only a week at sea and on his first trip out they were already saying he was bad luck. Some were saying that he was the reason that they weren't finding any fish. He was a liability, a Jonah. And soon, in about two minutes time, he would commit the greatest crime of all—a crime almost worse than murder. At least, to the crew of the *Raider* . . .

Only ten days ago, Laurie had been sitting with inky fingers at a school desk drawing maps in geography.

Now he was at the frozen top of the world, unable to stay upright on decks slimed with fish guts.

'Where's them needles?'

Every time the *Raider* took a sea, it wrenched Laurie off his feet. Even the veteran deckhands were sliding about in the fish pounds. It was a crazy schedule, hauling up and shooting the trawl every half hour in God-awful weather, with ice strung out like tattered crystal flags along the rigging. But the Iceman decreed it. So the crew worked like men possessed.

It was madness on deck. Fishing in the gathering dark with floodlights rigged to the foremast. Only the Iceman would risk his crew this way. Anything to give him the edge and send the *Raider* speeding home with every spare inch of her fishroom filled. There were top prices waiting for the first ship home. And when you sailed with the Iceman you earned a fortune. If you survived the trip.

It was bad enough for the experienced men. But for Laurie, a deckie-learner and useless at his job, it was like being dropped straight into hell.

The trawl net exploded out of the sea, a great, slithering, silver monster.

'The belly's ripped!'

'GIVE—ME—A—NEEDLE!'

That was the third hand, bawling at Laurie through the wind. The Iceman was howling something from the bridge but Laurie was dizzy, weak with sickness and fatigue. He couldn't connect. He could see their mouths moving but his head couldn't make sense of what they were saying. It had been twenty hours on, four hours off (if you were lucky) for the last three days. Meals when you could snatch them. And still they had hardly any fish. The Iceman had screwed up the tension until the men were almost crazy. But no one had cracked. Except for Laurie, new boy on board and the world's worst deckhand.

The wind screamed, waves belted the ship and a storm of seagulls screeched and fought all round her. Laurie reeled against the ship's rail and was flung back, clutching his side. Water streamed from his staggering figure and his needles, urgently needed to mend the net, skittered all over the deck.

'Christ! Christ!' screamed the mate, demented. 'Get below, you useless little git!'

And all the time the Iceman was looking down from the bridge like God. Laurie knew this, even though he hadn't seen his face since they started trawling three days ago.

The mate pulled back his arm and hit Laurie open-handed across the mouth. The Iceman saw him do it.

'Get below!' screamed the mate again like a maniac. 'Do you know what you've gone and done? You've stopped the trawl! Nobody *ever* stops the trawl on the *Raider*!'

The mate's glove, a solid lump of ice, sheered through Laurie's flesh and opened up his cheek. But Laurie didn't feel it, didn't even resent it. It was only what he deserved, for holding up the trawl. And the Iceman, looking down like God, agreed. As if the mate was the agent of his divine anger.

'Get that trawl net out! There's not much fishing time left!'

The few fish they'd caught were stiff, frozen before they hit the deck. Soon the sea would begin to freeze around them and even the Iceman would have to run for shelter.

Christmas Day out on the fishing grounds. And still no luck. The Iceman was losing his edge. Unthinkable that he should take the *Raider* home after the other ships and with only half her fishroom filled. Behind the frosty windows of the bridge the crew saw him pacing, pacing, watching the echo sounder, not eating or sleeping. Living on adrenalin. And the tension on board was charged and charged again until the deck, the cabin, the steel plates of the *Raider* seemed electric with it. As if, if you reached out to touch a bulkhead, it would hiss and crackle with a million volts.

Laurie was being punished. He was crouched by the rail filling needles with twine. You needed both hands to do this. He had no free hand to hold the rail even though the *Raider* was bucking through heavy seas. But he dared not stop. It was dark and dinner time. But, 'No Christmas dinner,' the mate had told him, 'till you get them needles filled.'

'You, Jonah,' one of the crew had hissed at him. 'This was going to be a record trip. The Iceman's greatest trip ever. More money than we've ever made! He staked his reputation on it. But you held up the trawl. You put Billy out of action. And he's worth twenty of you. A thousand of you!'

Laurie, his hands frozen, couldn't keep up with the rhythm of the gutting team. He'd slowed them down and, worse than that, his gutting knife had slipped into Billy's thigh. Billy couldn't work and now they were scared his blood was poisoned.

'We'll be a joke,' the third hand said, 'when we get back to port. Last and with no fish. The Iceman will be a joke. And all because of *you*.'

Laurie crouched by the rail, filling needles. His hands were cracked and bleeding with salt-water sores. It was Christmas Day—but he dared not let himself think about that.

Before he sailed he'd planned to keep a journal, a 'Seafarer's Journal'. Write up his adventures on the *Arctic Raider*, day by day: the first glacier, the first spouting whale, the first volcanic island. The night before he sailed he'd written a long, long entry. But he'd scarcely written anything since.

For a week before he sailed he'd secretly soaked his hands in methylated spirits to harden them. He'd done press-ups and sit-ups in his room to make himself tough and strong.

But he'd started being sick before they'd cleared the lock gates. He'd let a cable slip and almost sheared off the tip of the third hand's skull—neat as topping your breakfast egg. And on his first day, he'd shovelled ice for only an hour in the fishroom before he fell asleep and someone else had to finish the job. As junior deckhand he'd been a total disaster area.

They were having Christmas dinner in the galley. There was warm, fragrant steam coming up through the vents. But out here the ship was icing up. Laurie screwed up his eyes, tried to brush the ice-crystals off his eyelashes. He was swaying, dizzy, tired to the marrow of his bones. He had to jerk his head upright to stop himself falling face down in the basket of wooden needles and going to sleep.

His surroundings seemed unreal, shuddering in and out of focus. For a brief moment the engine's whine, the battering waves, the wind, faded into the background and

4

he saw the *Raider*, iced up like a Christmas cake, with a glittering superstructure and those icicles like tattered crystal flags along the rigging. And the sea around seemed full of silver coins as it too began to freeze.

'Beautiful,' murmured Laurie. 'Beautiful.'

But the *Raider* plunged down and took a sea and Laurie had to grab the basket to stop it falling over the side.

'Thank God.' He closed his eyes in silent prayer because he'd saved the needles. Then he opened them. This was reality.

Suddenly, Laurie spewed up into the needles. The next one he took out was coated with slime. It slithered from his frozen hands and was lost over the side.

Laurie had to account personally to the mate for every one of the needles in that basket.

In unthinking panic, he leapt up to peer over the rail and at that moment the *Raider* rolled and tipped him over the side into the dark. His basket of needles followed him. The ship rose up like a cliff face above him and he knew there was no one on deck. No one to see him fall or hear his cries. His only chance was to grab the rail as it came plunging down towards him slowly, slowly like a slow-motion film.

He stretched out both his arms, streaming with water.

Someone did see him fall. The Iceman was on his bridge, looking down. He saw the boy go over the side and when he didn't come back with the next wave he knew he was done for. Two, three minutes, was the most you could survive in that freezing sea and by the time they eased down, turned back, and in the dark—there wasn't a hope in hell, even of finding a body. He would have eased down if there'd been any hope at all. But in the circumstances it would be time wasted.

So the *Raider* steamed away to the best trip, with the best catches, that the Iceman had ever made. His reputation, in his home port, became even more spectacular. They made up songs about his exploits. Some said he had supernatural powers, because he always knew where to find the fish. Some said he'd sold his soul to the devil.

But the Iceman didn't know everything. He saw a great many things from the bridge. He saw his deckhand fall but he knew nothing of the conscious, clear-minded decision that Laurie took to let go of the rail. Laurie had the rail in his hands and it was taking him up, up again to the deck of the *Raider*.

He could have saved himself. But he chose not to. Instead Laurie unclenched his fingers, let the rail go—and slipped back into the icy waters.

1

Madeleine pulled chewing gum from her mouth in a long elastic string, then let it twang back. She kicked her leg out restlessly. The toe cap of her Doc Martens clanged off a metal table leg. One of the library staff eyed her over half-moon specs.

Silly cow, thought Maddy as she ruffled the pages of a book, pretending to study. It was worse than being at school.

She flicked past an old photograph. It was a grey and grainy print of the Iceman being presented with a trophy, the Silver Cod. Behind him crowded the crew of the *Arctic Raider* (minus Laurie). 'Skipper of the Year 1952' it said beneath the picture. There were more words, but Maddy didn't read them. The photo didn't interest her at all.

She decided she was allergic to reference libraries. The staleness, the hush, the drugged clock dragging round, the dreary air of time suspended . . .

'God, I'm sooo *bored*!' Maddy sighed: 'Huhhh!' Her breath made her notebook pages flutter. That made her laugh. She crammed a fist between her teeth to stop the giggles bubbling over. She hated this silence and solemnity—it made her think morbid thoughts. It made her think of death.

An old man with a skull-like face twisted round to glare at her.

What's he looking at? thought Maddy.

She sharpened her pencil, wrenching it around in her pink Cadillac sharpener, watching the clean wood shavings twist on to the table top. She'd sharpened it five times already. Soon, she reflected, it would be completely sharpened away. Then she couldn't make any more notes. Good.

She checked her make-up in the shiny top of her pencil tin. Am I too orange? she thought. Her new cover-up stick had a suspiciously orange tinge.

She twisted the gold studs round in her ears. And winced. She had just had them pierced for the second time.

'Jee-sus,' she growled softly to herself. 'I'm going crazy!'

She resented with all her heart and soul having to be here in this library. She resented it for lots of reasons. Maddy checked off the reasons on her fingers:

1. It was December 20th, the Christmas holidays. No one should have to sit in a stuffy library and do history projects at Christmas. Especially when the shopping malls were at their most lively, most glittering. Especially when the project was called: 'The Decline of the Local Fishing Industry 1950–1995'. Just thinking of it made Maddy slump into a coma.

2. No one should have to work with people who weren't their friends. The history teacher, mean bitch, had split the class up into pairs. Deliberately not let anyone choose who to work with.

And Maddy had ended up partnered with a complete nobody. Teamed up with a girl so low in the class popularity ratings that Maddy hardly knew her name. Flora, the girl she was stuck with, had been in the same class as Maddy for four years. But Maddy's only impression of her, after all that time, was of a white, anxious face, a thick fringe of hair and fat legs. Yet the two of them were supposed to research this assignment together! Flora was supposed to be meeting her here, in this library, at eleven o'clock.

Nuts to that, thought Maddy.

She had no intention of co-operating. It would destroy her image, being seen in town with someone so uncool, so lacking in style and status—and named after a brand of low-fat margarine. Come to think of it, Maddy had never seen Flora in town. She had never seen her anywhere outside school.

Maybe she crawls under a stone, thought Maddy with a guilty snicker at her own cruelty.

Was this the third reason? Maddy had lost count. The *third* reason she resented being here was: for the first time in her life Maddy had the house to herself. For one night. Unbelievable. It had been touch and go. Her parents had had serious doubts. But after a flurry of negotiations Maddy had gained the upper hand. ('I can't possibly come, can I? I've got this project to do. And it's very important— it's part of my exam assessment.')

So they'd gone off, with her little brother, on an emergency visit to a sick grandma and left her at home alone. On condition that she completed her project and didn't have any parties.

Nuts to that, Maddy had thought, during a wild, stomping dance of self-congratulation. She'd already alerted all her friends.

But her parents had been cunning. They had set up a network of neighbours, librarians, and other spies, to 'keep an eye on her' and report back.

'Just to make sure I don't have any fun,' grumbled Maddy.

They had only been gone since 7 a.m. Yet, already, they had phoned from a motorway service station, interrupting her when she was busy in the bathroom, putting blonde streaks in her hair.

'Stop checking up on me,' Maddy told them, down the phone. 'I'm all right!'

And, worst of all, to make sure she had no time to get into trouble, they'd fixed up an interview with some old fisherman. 'You'll get some great material for your project,' they'd said, keenly.

It was just like them. They had to interfere. As if they didn't trust her to sort things out herself.

Maddy was tempted to give the interview a miss. But she wanted to keep her parents sweet. Then they might go away and leave her in charge of the house again one day. And next time, she might have a boyfriend to take full advantage of the opportunity. She'd just dumped her present one—very bad timing.

Winter sun streamed in through the venetian blinds, making the dust specks dance and sparkle.

Aarggh! Maddy screamed, inside her head.

She'd had enough. She couldn't stand this place a moment longer. She'd been good, tried to do as her parents suggested—find information for her project from local history books. She had tried. But this pile of books about the fishing industry with their fuzzy photographs of trawlers and endless lists of record catches just made her eyes cloudy with boredom. Only four facts had hooked themselves, like tiny spiky seeds, on to her memory:

1. When you were fishing in Arctic waters snot froze into green icicles as it dripped out of your nose. You had to snap them off.
2. A man had been sliced clean in two by a warp going at 120 m.p.h. that split and whipped across the deck.
3. On the old steam trawlers there were no toilets. Men dangled their bare bottoms over the side. 'This was very difficult,' the book had said, 'especially when the vessel was pitching and rolling.'
4. One boat, the *Arctic Raider*, was more famous than all the others.

That was enough research for today. Gunshots ricocheted around the room. It was Maddy, slamming all her books shut. Skullface looked up. Maddy grinned sweetly at him. Knowing the librarian was watching her, she took the gum out of her mouth and stuck it underneath the table. Time to go.

'Five, four, three, two, one!' She counted down the seconds to eleven o'clock. 'That's it, then. She's had her chance. She's obviously not coming.'

Relieved, she sprang out of her seat and waded through the hush, thick as molasses, towards the library door. She was anxious to escape before Flora turned up.

Being seen with Flora, in public, would destroy her

credibility. Flora never seemed to be involved in anything important that was going on. Maddy couldn't imagine being like that. Her phone line was always buzzing—with invitations, intrigues, talk about boys. If she didn't come to school, friends would phone up and say, 'Where were you today?' If Flora didn't turn up neither Maddy or her friends would notice. She could be absent for weeks, dead even, before any of them would comment on it. Flora was so far outside Maddy's orbit that she might have been in another galaxy.

Outside the library Maddy took a deep breath of petrol fumes and felt revived.

'Thank Christ I'm out of there.'

She ducked down a subway. She thought that it was the best way to avoid bumping into Flora. She was wrong. If Maddy had cared at all about Flora's life outside school, if she had bothered to find out anything about her, she would have known that subways were exactly the kind of place where you might bump into her. Subways, alleyways, back streets, waste ground: these were Flora's natural territory.

2

Maddy couldn't understand how she'd got herself into this mess. She didn't usually end up doing anything she didn't want to—yet here she was stumbling behind a wheezing old woman up a cramped stairway to the attics of a Victorian house. And she had no idea why.

She had planned to spend thirty minutes, maximum, tolerating the ramblings of Mr Pederson, the old fisherman she'd been sent to interview. Then she would tell him some lie or other ('I must go! I've got a dentist's appointment in twenty minutes.') and make her escape. She had it all worked out. But things had got badly out of control.

Ten minutes ago his wife had shown her in. Nothing threatening there. Maddy had glanced at Mrs Pederson and dismissed her as the grandma-type: plump, grey-haired, glasses, like a million other old women.

'I'm Madeleine.' She'd introduced herself briskly. 'You don't know me. But my mum rang you the other day. I've come to interview Mr Pederson. For my school history project.'

She had followed Mrs Pederson through the house to a living room. There were many doors and narrow corridors where you cracked your hipbone on dark and heavy furniture. Probably, this had once been a boarding house. It was near the sea. You could see chilly grey waves from some of the windows. But Maddy hadn't felt uneasy. She was a confident person. And anyway, she was too busy thinking about what treats to buy herself for lunch. She just wanted to get this over with and hit the shops.

'He won't be long,' Mrs Pederson had said. 'He's in his workshop, out in the garden.'

And Maddy had sat down. She'd decided to make it clear to Mrs Pederson that her time was precious. So she'd pulled up her cuff and, frowning slightly, peered beneath it as if she was checking her watch. Although she knew quite well that she wasn't wearing one.

But it had worked, of course. It always did. 'Are you in a hurry?' Mrs Pederson had asked.

'Well,' Maddy shook her head regretfully, 'I've got a dentist's appointment in twenty minutes. Got this terrible toothache . . .' Maddy had cradled her cheek and looked brave.

Unlike a typical grandma, Mrs Pederson didn't cluck in sympathy. Instead she'd said, 'Tell you what. You came about the old days, didn't you, about the fishing? I can show you something. I can show you something interesting, while you're waiting.'

So now Maddy was following her upstairs. To the first storey, to the second and still upwards. She noticed, as Mrs Pederson turned round, that her face was flushed with an alarming vitality. That her voice, between rattling gasps for breath, was becoming more urgent and excited. She's a sick old woman, Maddy thought. What's she playing at, dragging me up stairs like this?

'We're nearly there. We're nearly at the top.'

The entrance to the last stairway was a black slit in the wall. Mrs Pederson plunged into it. And, for the first time, Maddy felt a twist of sick fear. It was fear from her childhood, of the dark at the top of the stairs.

'Where are we going?' she called up anxiously, into the shadows.

'To the attics,' came a faint and weary voice. 'We're going to the attics.'

Maddy stamped on her fluttery feelings of panic, as you might crush an insect. She didn't approve of panicking. It was too uncool.

'Come on,' she sneered at her own hesitation, 'you're not still scared of the dark, are you?' It blipped through her mind that, when she was small, she'd been scared that her hand would flop out of the covers while she was asleep. And the monster under the bed would gnaw it down to the bone.

13

And she would wake up with a skeleton claw waggling on the end of her arm . . .

'For Chrissake!' Grinning at her own childish terrors, she trudged up the narrow steps. The scarlet sworls of the carpet and the thick brass stair-rods gleamed dimly at her through the gloom.

Mrs Pederson was on a tiny landing, clutching the railings, waiting for her. Behind her was a door.

'Are you all right?' said Maddy, concerned. For the first time she really looked at Mrs Pederson. There was sweat on her forehead and upper lip. And her face had a grey sheen, like putty. She plucked at her cardigan, as if her chest hurt her. But her eyes, behind those grandma's specs, were triumphant.

'I haven't been up here,' she said to Maddy breathlessly, 'for such a long time. I'm not supposed to come up here. It's my heart, see. I'm not supposed to climb these stairs.'

'Let's go down then,' Maddy found herself begging. She wasn't in the habit of begging people to do things. But the state Mrs Pederson was in unnerved her. She hated morbid things like illness. 'You can show me another time.'

'No!' With supreme self-will Mrs Pederson straightened up her contorted body. 'I'm all right. Really, I'm all right now.' And she did sound revived. Her voice was light, almost girlish.

'Well, OK,' said Maddy, still flustered. She checked that non-existent watch. 'But I can't stay long. I've got to talk to Mr Pederson yet. I mean, that's what I came for, really.'

But Mrs Pederson was already pushing back the door. It only opened a little, as if there was some obstacle behind it. There was just enough room for Mrs Pederson to slide through the gap.

For a moment Maddy hung back, stranded on the landing. Below her was the stairwell, dark as a bottomless pool. There was nowhere else to go but forward, into the attics.

So she sidled through the door.

Straight into a world of nets and sunshine.

She bounced off a fishing-net wall: 'What the hell—?'

Bewildered, dazzled, Maddy looked up. Dusty sunshine was tangled in net hammocks slung above her head. The meshes were orange nylon, glowing ruby in the light.

'Mrs Pederson? Where are you?'

This vast attic, big as a ballroom, lit from above by skylights, was festooned with fishing nets. A maze of nets, a honeycomb—swags of them hung from the walls, screens of them across the room made tunnels, alleyways, and chambers.

Maddy turned back towards the door, her only escape route. But a curtain of net had fallen over it and she couldn't find a way out. Disorientated, she stumbled against the first net screen. It rippled and flimsy model planes tied into it rattled gently like windchimes. Bits of wing and fuselage fell off around her feet.

'What the hell's going on? Mrs Pederson? Mrs Pederson?'

Maddy stood at the threshold of the net labyrinth, peering through the meshes into its secret depths, scared of advancing in case it sucked her in.

'Mrs Pederson!' She could hear a shrill edge of panic in her cry. It didn't sound like her voice at all.

'I'm here.'

From nowhere, Mrs Pederson appeared, smiling, calm, with sunlight frizzing her grey hair into glittering silver wires.

'It's all right,' she said. 'Don't be afraid. I made this room. I made it after my son Laurie died.'

'Who?' said Maddy, mystified.

Mrs Pederson tugged gently at her sleeve. 'Come on. It's all right. You're not trapped. You can walk between the nets. You can walk all around the room between the nets. If you know the way.'

Maddy frowned. Normality was turned upon its head. She couldn't deal with it. 'I don't understand. What is this place?'

Stuck into the net was a wooden braiding needle, like the shuttle weavers use, loaded with twine. It was a needle like this that Laurie lost from the decks of the *Arctic Raider*.

'I learned to braid nets when I was a girl,' Mrs Pederson was telling her, chattily, as if this was a completely normal situation. 'My mother taught me. Lots of people in this town used to make trawl nets in their houses. It's not unusual.'

Not unusual! If she hadn't been so worried, Maddy would have snorted with laughter. As it was, she felt herself relaxing, just a little. But not very much—because it had just occurred to her that Mrs Pederson was crazy.

'You're telling me you made all this?' asked Maddy, cautiously. 'You made this room of nets?'

'It took me years.' There was pride in Mrs Pederson's voice.

Maddy looked around. She still didn't know what to make of it. The sun slid further into the room, bleaching the coarse twine, making the hairs on it glitter as if each rope was sheathed in fuzzy gold. She saw now that trapped in the mesh, braided into it, were all kinds of objects. All the way through the net jungle she could see colours, shapes, dangling like Christmas tree decorations. And from its meshy heart she caught a flash of blue, like a secret pool in the middle of a forest. But she couldn't tell from here what it was.

'Very nice,' murmured Maddy, becoming more and more convinced that she was with a mad woman. She still felt totally confused, as if she'd been yanked out of everyday life by the scruff of her neck and dragged kicking and protesting into a crazy world.

She looked at her ghost watch. 'Got to go,' she muttered. 'Got to go now.'

But Mrs Pederson, eyes gleaming with a frightening enthusiasm, ignored her plea. 'Come on,' she said. 'I'll show you the way through.' And she vanished, into a gap in the net wall that Maddy hadn't seen.

'Come on.' Her silver head appeared again and she

pulled the net aside, like the doorway to a tent. And Maddy, not knowing what else to do, ducked through. The braided wall fell neatly back into place. There was no gap any more, no retreat. And now she was enclosed by this mysterious pavilion, with its swooping net roof. She was in the first of its many tunnels, that led, like connecting corridors, to the far end of the attic. She hastened after Mrs Pederson, afraid that, if she lost her guide, she might never find her way out.

And suddenly, Maddy found herself face to face with all kinds of photos, tucked into the net. Old photos, cracked and yellow—one of a gummy baby propped on lacy pillows, another of a pudgy-kneed schoolboy in short trousers with a blazer and cap and a new satchel shiny as a horse-chestnut. Another of the same boy, in football strip with his foot upon a leather football.

Locks of curly, blond hair were threaded through the mesh. Mrs Pederson paused to stroke them. Maddy shivered. She'd already guessed whose hair that was. It was the hair of Mrs Pederson's dead son.

'That's Laurie's hair,' said Mrs Pederson, as if she could read her thoughts. 'From his first haircut. He had lovely hair when he was a baby—come through here.'

And again, she shook out a fold in the mesh to reveal a door. Dazed, Maddy followed. As they pushed through, the nets swayed and billowed, throwing shifting lozenges of light on to the floor and walls. Above her head, thin metal sheets of Meccano tinkled.

In this tunnel there were other, stranger objects: a child's red woollen glove, a yellow stub of pencil, a green and yellow school scarf, the brown leather football from the photo swinging, creaking gently, in its own braided hammock.

Maddy, in her confusion, fell against the rope wall making it bulge and rock. Receding depths of mesh shuddered in sympathy as if the whole room was a single breathing organism. Unseen objects rustled. Something clunked down and rolled along the floor. It was a glass marble with swirls of green and blue inside it. Maddy

17

looked up. There was a braided bag of them dangling above her head. They clicked together as she passed beneath them.

'And look,' said Mrs Pederson. 'Here's my Laurie's school reports. He got very good school reports.'

These down-to-earth words seemed to bring Maddy back to sanity. Her mind stopped whirling. She'd already guessed what this room was. It was some kind of shrine to a dead son. Here were collected his photographs and childhood toys and possessions. Even locks of his hair. All arranged in this creepy fishing-net memorial.

'Grief,' Maddy told herself in the most matter-of-fact voice she could manage, 'grief does funny things to people.' She desperately needed to find some logical explanation for the bizarre situation she found herself in. She had heard of people who left dead sons' and daughters' rooms untouched for years and years with every possession in the same place. Well, this wasn't much different from that, was it? Not much.

'When did he die?' she asked Mrs Pederson. 'Your son? What did you say his name was?'

'Laurie, his name was Laurie. And he died in 1953. He was lost overboard from a trawler.'

So long ago! It seemed to Maddy like ancient history.

'He was lost overboard,' continued Mrs Pederson, 'from the *Arctic Raider*.'

'Wait a minute!' Maddy felt much better now, almost back in control. 'I've read about that ship, the *Arctic Raider*. I read about her in the library, just this morning. She was a famous ship!' Just thinking about the boredom of the reference library seemed to flush a cold blast of normality through her brain. Calmer now, she read Laurie's school reports, crisp and yellowing with age, as if she wasn't standing in a cat's cradle of mesh, a gigantic net cocoon.

'Pleasing, capable, conscientious,' the reports read.

'He was very clever,' said Mrs Pederson. 'Too clever to go to sea. I didn't want him to. But he loved the sea. He was

18

born to it, like his dad. He loved it on the *Arctic Raider*. She was his very first boat.'

For the first time, Maddy felt the sadness of it all. Standing here, with a drowned boy's childhood fixed as if in amber all around her.

'He was my only son,' said Mrs Pederson, as they walked on. 'My only child. I didn't want him to go. Because, when they come back, when boys come back from their first trip to sea, they've changed. You've lost them. They don't talk to their mothers any more. "If you send a boy to hell," they used to say round here, "you can't expect him to come back an angel." But I couldn't stop him going. He loved the sea. And it wasn't hell on board the *Raider* for him. It was heaven. He loved being a deckie-learner—loved his job. When they came back, after he was lost, the rest of the crew told me that. Born to the sea, they said he was, a natural trawlerman, like his dad.'

Maddy listened to the soothing sound of Mrs Pederson's voice. Fascinated, she watched rhomboids of light pirouetting round her head. It was peaceful here, serene. Like walking, she imagined, on the ocean floor with sunlight filtering down.

When she touched the net the ripples spread like waves. Somewhere in the distance some object, another toy belonging to Mrs Pederson's long-dead son, chimed melodically. Well, Maddy was thinking, there's no harm in all this, is there? It's a bit weird. But there's no harm in it, really.

'January 3rd he was lost,' Mrs Pederson was saying as if she was talking in a trance. 'Just a day away from home, after their best trip ever. A record trip it was. If only Laurie had been there to get that trophy with them. He would have been that proud. But at least he helped with the trawling, he helped to land the catches. He worked as good as any of the men. They told me that, told me how well-liked he was. He had a lovely Christmas Day, with a proper Christmas dinner, Christmas pudding and everything. And he saw the New Year in. Just as good as if he'd been at home. I know all this, you see, I know about his last days because Laurie wasn't on his own aboard that ship. He was sailing with—'

'Wait a minute,' Maddy interrupted. 'How old was Laurie when he got lost at sea?'

She had stopped short in front of a photograph, fixed like the others, in the net wall. It was a strange photo: it showed the *Raider*, deadly grey predator of Arctic waters, slinking through the lock gates. While up in the right-hand corner, grinning down like the man in the moon, was inset a boy's face—Laurie's face.

Mrs Pederson turned back. 'That photo is the last one I've got of Laurie. It's him with his first boat. All the young lads used to get photos like that made up, to give to their mothers or their girlfriends. Laurie got that done especially for me.'

I'll bet he did, thought Maddy with sudden cynicism. She was studying Laurie's face. He wasn't bad-looking. But she didn't fancy him. Not her type.

'So how old was he?'

'He was sixteen when he died. Just turned sixteen,' said Mrs Pederson.

'Sixteen!' Maddy almost said: 'You're kidding!' For the eager fresh-faced boy grinning from the picture did not look sixteen. He didn't look as if he had to shave yet. He still had slightly chubby cheeks, as if he hadn't lost the puppy fat of childhood.

And this room of nets, with its marbles, model planes, and footballs, seemed like a little boy's memorial. He must have been, she decided, very immature.

Her sympathy for Laurie began to leak away. His tragedy didn't seem half so poignant now that she suspected how uncool he'd been, what a mummy's boy he was. The spell of the room of nets was breaking. 'And what's this?' she said with some irritation, tapping at a faded school notebook dangling from the mesh. The room was quiet now—it didn't speak to her any more. In fact, she could hear the growl of cars going by outside on the road. She had lost interest.

20

'I'll have to go now,' she said. 'I'll have to see Mr Pederson another time.'

But Mrs Pederson was still locked into memories of her dead son. 'That's Laurie's Seafarer's Journal,' she answered Maddy.

'What?' said Maddy, frowning with impatience. Now she looked more closely she could just make out those faded words, SEAFARER'S JOURNAL, written on the front in capitals. They were coloured in in blue wax crayon and wavy, like the sea. She could have guessed that Laurie had done that.

'I found it in his kitbag,' explained Mrs Pederson. 'When the *Raider* came home, they brought me back Laurie's kitbag that he took on board with him. And that notebook was wrapped up in a jumper. It's his diary, his secret diary.'

'Oh yeah,' said Maddy, faintly interested. She opened it. She wouldn't have been surprised to see it printed out, in a neat childish hand. That would support the opinions she was rapidly forming about Laurie's character. But the writing wasn't neat. It was a large, untidy scrawl.

December 13th, Maddy read, 1952.

My name is Laurie Pederson and I'm 16 today and one day I'm going to be a top skipper. I'm going to be the youngest trawler skipper ever.

Tomorrow, I'm going to sea on the *Arctic Raider* as a deckie-learner. Mum doesn't want me to go. She says that I should stay at school, get a good shore job, a teacher or something. But I'm not going back to school. My dad left school when he was 14. He started out as a trimmer chopping coal down the stokehold. And it never did him any harm. Look where he is today. He says no mothers want their sons to go to sea. But they go anyway, if they're not soft that is. And anyway, Mum will be calmed down by the time I come back. I'll buy her a really nice present, a brooch or something, with my money. You earn really good wages on the *Raider*. I'm lucky to start out on that boat.

21

It's a dead hard life at sea and dangerous. Everybody knows that. But it's going to be the best adventure ever. We'll go to Norway, the White Sea, Greenland, Iceland, Bear Island, where there's icebergs and glaciers and waves high as mountains. And I've made this serious promise, to write in this Seafarer's Journal every day, to keep a proper record of my first trip out. The first iceberg that I see, the first whale, the first volcano. Sometimes off Iceland when a volcano erupts whole islands come out of the sea and then sink back again. I've read about it. I'm going to write it all down. So I remember my first trip for the rest of my life.

I should get some sleep. But I can't. I'm too excited and that's why I'm still writing even though it's two in the morning and the house is quiet. Mum and Dad are asleep. When I write in this Journal tomorrow I'll be writing it aboard the *Arctic Raider*!! I'll be in my bunk on the *Raider*!! But I won't have time to write this much because I'll be busy. I'll—

Maddy flicked the book shut. She didn't need to read any more. She was unimpressed. His enthusiasm, all those exclamation marks, made him sound naïve. A dork, she thought automatically. If he'd been in my class he would be one of the dorks. Flora and him would make a good pair.

Then, on second thoughts, she reached out and thumbed through the notebook. That first entry was Laurie's last. There seemed to be nothing else written at all.

'He didn't keep his promise then,' she pointed out to Mrs Pederson. 'He didn't keep a record of his first trip.'

'Ah well,' said Mrs Pederson, 'he was too busy, wasn't he, too excited. He was enjoying himself too much.'

As if Maddy wasn't there, she took a wooden needle out of the pocket of her apron and began to braid, repairing a tear in the net. 'There's lots of different knots in braiding,' she was saying, 'there's the Bridport knot, the reef knot, the double sheet bend—'

Maddy pressed her fingertips against her eyelids. She felt

22

herself growing dizzy. Mrs Pederson, with her frizzy silver hair, her body speckled with gold light, was going in and out of focus like a genie shrinking back then escaping from its bottle. As she worked, the nets swayed, then distant nets shuddered in response. Colours whirled like a mad kaleidoscope: blues, greens, the red of Laurie's woolly glove. And the room began to whisper, rustle, sigh along with the rhythm of the nets.

I've had enough of this! thought Maddy, rubbing at her eyes to make the movement stop, to make the room click back into focus. I must be mad! She couldn't believe that she was really here, walking through a fishing-net shrine to a boy who drowned more than forty years ago.

'I have to go,' she insisted.

'That's a shame.' Mrs Pederson sounded disappointed. 'There's more to see. There's all the badges Laurie got at wolf cubs. And his first baby shoes—'

'No!' Maddy's cry of revulsion startled them both. 'I can't stay here any longer.'

But she'd lost all sense of direction. She couldn't remember how to get back to the door. She ran along the screen, scrabbling at the mesh to try and find its secret openings. Laurie's school reports fluttered to the ground like pale leaves. His football creaked in its net cradle like someone creeping behind her in new leather shoes.

'You're going the wrong way,' said Mrs Pederson, slipping the wooden needle back in her apron pocket. The effort of climbing steep stairs and lifting her arm to braid had put a strain upon her diseased heart. She felt pain clenching in her chest. But she didn't care. It was worth it just to be in Laurie's room again.

Maddy scarcely knew how she escaped from that house. She recalled clattering back down dark stairs. There was a hurried leavetaking conversation with Mrs Pederson. But she couldn't remember what was said. And she wasn't aware of the deathly pallor on Mrs Pederson's face as she stood in the doorway waving goodbye.

As Maddy rushed through the backyard, she glimpsed

Mr Pederson, the man she'd come to interview, crouched over a bench in his workshop. He was making something—but she couldn't see what it was. When she passed by, he raised his head—grey eyes, grey hair, lean, deeply-lined face. He seemed surprised to see her. But she didn't stop.

She was half-way down the street before she realized that she was running. Self-consciously, she slowed to a halt.

'Come on,' she mocked herself. 'Nothing's happened to you. You're all right, aren't you?' But this evening, when her parents phoned, she would tell them about Mrs Pederson. She would make sure they felt guilty for sending her to see a mad woman. 'Hang on,' she reconsidered, 'better not worry them. They might decide to come back.' She didn't want to jeopardize her precious night of freedom. 'Don't say anything!' she warned herself. And anyway, even in the heart of the room of nets, Mrs Pederson had not seemed mad. She had seemed ordinary. Somehow, that made her even more disturbing.

It was a clear blue day, crisp and bitter cold. Maddy found herself taking a short cut along the beach back to the shopping centre. The tide was low and the mud-flats glittered with a slick and poisonous sheen right out to the horizon. She kicked a rotting life jacket out of her way. Debris scattered the tideline: smashed wooden fishboxes, the round metal bobbins that once upon a time were strung like beads on trawl nets, smashed fish baskets—she'd read about those.

'They used to hoist one of those up the rigging to show they were trawling. See?' she told herself. 'You've learned something for your project.' She hadn't, she considered, learned anything of value at Mrs Pederson's. It had been a waste of time.

In fact, it seemed so unreal that it could all have been a bizarre dream . . . Without thinking, Maddy picked a curl of hair off her coat: white-blond hair, fine and silky. Not her hair. She stroked it, puzzled.

'Ugh!' Grimacing, she shook her arm wildly, as if some repulsive insect had landed there. She had recognized

Laurie's hair, brushed off the nets and still clinging to her sleeve.

Careless of the pain, she slapped at her own arm, until every wisp of hair was gone and there was no trace of Laurie left.

'For God's sake!' she scolded herself out loud, shocked at her own over-reaction.

Her voice echoed in the wide empty spaces.

She wished she'd never taken this short cut. It was so quiet here. She glanced nervously over her shoulder. There was no movement. Except in the creeks that wormed through the mud-flats, where water slopped round algal-green timber columns.

She'd reached the breaker's yard where they used to bring ships to be stripped and gutted. It was closed now—the men and cranes and cutting gear all gone. But the mud-flats around it were studded with metal like a biker's jacket. There were old diesel engines, metal plates, funnels, hulls. This was where she turned off, crossed the disused railway line and walked through a subway into the town centre.

There was the hulk of a trawler. Maddy wasn't interested in it. Dozens of trawlers had been broken up here since the fishing industry collapsed. She veered off to the left towards the old railway line. And that was when she happened to catch sight of the name on the hull of the wrecked boat. They were corroded, worn away, but the huge white letters were still visible.

They said: *ARCTIC RAIDER.*

3

At ten thirty that morning, when Maddy was wondering, Am I too orange? in the library, Flora was hard at work on their project. She was talking to a neighbour, Mr Walters, about the old days, when the town was a busy fishing port.

She had a book open on her knee, ready to take notes. Underneath the book, shoving it with its head, was Mr Walters' old dog. To her embarrassment, it had wriggled up on its belly and dug its head between her knees. She scratched behind its scabby ears. It whined and shivered.

This room oppressed her: all dreary browns and greys with a musty, doggy smell. The gas fire made her drowsy. Outside, in the winter sunshine, the lawn sparkled, crunchy with white frost . . . Flora jerked upright in her chair. The dog whined in protest as her knees squeezed its thin head like an almond in nutcrackers. She'd forgotten it was there. Must pay attention.

'So, Mr Walters,' she said brightly, 'did you say that the last ship you worked on was the *Arctic Raider*?'

It was the only thing she'd written down, five minutes ago, in large unsteady letters because of that shuffling dog. Since then she'd written nothing—except she'd decorated the name *Arctic Raider*, with some wavy lines underneath it. She'd clicked her pen on to blue to do that. She had one of those fat pens that contain several colours . . . Pay attention!

Mr Walters had a pitted strawberry nose. Maddy would have thought, Why doesn't he do something about those blackheads? A Bodyshop facial scrub or something? But Flora was too uneasy with her own appearance to be critical of other people's. She couldn't help noticing though, how Mr Walters' lower lip, thick and pink as a slab of pork, drooped and trembled when he got excited. He was excited now.

'That broke me, being on that ship. That finished me off, the *Arctic Raider* did. Like they finished off that poor boy—' His liver-spotted hand started quivering on the chair arm.

'What boy? What boy, Mr Walters?' Flora clicked her pen to red, ready to take important notes.

But the dog was poking his nose into the crotch of her jeans. Hot with embarrassment, she pushed him away. He cringed off and watched her from his dog basket.

'Christmas Day it was when that boy went over the side. That deckie-learner. I can't place the year exactly but it was when the *Raider* made her best trip ever. I remember that. But he was a bastard that skipper—'

'Bastard,' wrote Flora gravely in her notebook. 'Christmas Day', she wrote and 'Best Trip Ever'.

'He didn't even stop the ship.'

'Who didn't?'

'The Iceman, the Iceman didn't!' quavered Mr Walters. 'That's who I'm talking about! I'm talking about the skipper of the *Raider*.'

'I don't understand,' said Flora. 'Do you mean that this skipper never went back to look for the boy that fell overboard? Just let him drown?'

'He would have been dead anyway. Frozen to death—in them Arctic waters. But that wasn't the point. The point was . . . The point was . . . '

Mr Walters paused, his old face blank and sagging. He'd forgotten what the point was. His head sank into his chest. 'Only sixteen,' he mumbled, 'and we made his life hell.'

'What?' said Flora. She thought she must have misheard. 'What did you just say, Mr Walters?'

'Nobody cared. When the ship didn't turn back nobody cared. I ate his Christmas dinner . . . '

The only sound in the room was the gas fire, hissing. Flora waited. But Mr Walters had talked himself to a standstill.

She got up. Mr Walters jerked as if someone had just snapped their fingers and brought him out of a trance. 'Eh?'

he moaned. 'Eh?' Looking round bewildered, his slippery inner lip exposed.

He's forgotten who I am, thought Flora. The dog uncurled from its basket and grovelled up to her with a sly look on its face. Flora backed away.

But Mr Walters hadn't forgotten. 'Come again, Flora,' he was saying. 'I hardly ever get the chance to talk about the old days. Come round again.'

Flora thought, Not likely!—but she felt guilty about it. He was a lonely and confused old man. She felt guilty that her revulsion was stronger than her pity.

Outside his front door she breathed a great lungful of glittering winter air as if she'd just stepped out of prison. She looked at the few words written in her notebook, then shoved it away into her coat pocket. Nothing of value there. She would have liked to present Maddy, at the library, with some good research, as a sort of peace offering. Now she had nothing to take along but herself. And she knew Maddy wouldn't be impressed by that.

She wandered along the sea-shore, over the squelchy debris washed up by last night's tide. She was walking slowly, putting off the meeting with Maddy. She was really nervous about it, as if it was a test or examination that she was bound to fail.

The station clock tower caught her eye. The railway line was closed, the station boarded up, but the old clock kept on going. She stared, dismayed, at its curly iron hands. In disbelief she mouthed the time: 'Five to eleven!' She had no idea it was so late.

Five minutes left to reach the library. She could make it, just, if she took a short cut down Moravian Street.

But even thinking about Moravian Street made her face flush and her hands grow clammy. She stood there, dithering.

There must have been a time in her life when Moravian Street wasn't a threat to her. But she couldn't remember back that far. For Flora, the geography of the town was dominated by Moravian Street. The map of the town she carried in her head had a big dark star squatting in the middle of it. That was Moravian Street—and everything else revolved around it.

Moravian Street was Flora's no-go area, enemy territory. Yet it was an unremarkable street of town houses, just like a thousand others. And the reasons why Flora flinched every time she thought about it were unremarkable too. A story that must repeat itself every day in schools all over the globe. A story of friends becoming enemies, of trust betrayed. That kind of stuff. Flora could remember precisely when it started. The day when, for reasons she still didn't understand, her best friend became her tormentor.

They had been in the biology lab. It was sickly with escaped gas from Bunsen burners. Flora felt sleepy and faintly nauseous. But the paper pellet that stung the back of her neck had woken her up.

She turned round, ready to laugh at the joke but saw her friend teamed up with a giggling crony. They had little white balls of ammunition ranged up along the desk. Their faces were sneering and malicious.

That had been the beginning. Just that. But years of petty, spiteful harassment followed—name calling, stealing her books, following her home, tailing her with mocking grins. They never let her alone. She'd hoped they would get tired of it.

But they never did. They seemed obsessed with her, as if she was a habit they couldn't break, as if persecuting her was essential to their friendship.

It wasn't even persecution. Flora wouldn't have called it that: she would have thought that name was too dramatic. They jostled her in school corridors. But mostly they didn't touch her. They just mocked her for being fat, pathetic, a baby, a wimp. Flora almost wished that they would beat her up, break her nose or something so that at last people would notice and take action to stop it. But they never went that far. That was not their style. They just hounded her sneakily, with tedious persistence. Like water dripping on stone, they wore away her self-esteem until it was as thin and fragile as eggshells.

She didn't retaliate. She just skulked and scurried and hid behind lockers in school corridors—and avoided Moravian Street like the plague because that was where both of them lived. Once, at school, she had crammed herself under a teacher's desk, curled up like a foetus until they passed by. And she'd hated herself for her cowardice. 'You're really feeble,' she would tell herself. 'You deserve it! No wonder they never give up. You're such an easy target!'

She never gave herself any credit—not for the fact that she had steeled herself never to cry in front of them, or for the times she walked, stoically, with her head held high, while they capered around, insulting her. Or for the fact that she bore all this alone without telling anyone.

For years, they'd been like mocking, grinning shadows, constantly reinforcing her own poor opinion of herself. They ruled her life. They had her imprisoned as effectively as if she'd been in chains. At weekends, all her activities were restricted by the constant thought: Will they be there? Will they go swimming today? Will they be in town shopping? She stayed at home, most of the time, keeping well away from the windows. And when she did go out she sneaked through alleys, waste ground, backstreets so she didn't meet them.

Oddly, the few days when they did nothing at all were the most nerve-racking. For then the tension would be unbearable. They would pass behind her so close that she would cringe at their hot breath on her neck. Yet they would say nothing. They would swerve towards her in the corridor, but not crash into her. They wouldn't look once in her direction, as if she was invisible. It was almost a relief when one of them jeered, 'Get out of the way, fatty!' At least she knew that she existed again.

Flora hadn't told her parents. Her mother, harassed already by her three smaller brothers and sisters, would have seen Flora's problem as another burden in her life. She often said, 'What's wrong with you today? You look really miserable!' Yet Flora knew, if she confessed, her mother would fuss and fret and look so distressed that Flora would feel guilty for telling her. So Flora would answer, 'I'm all right.' And protect her mother from the real reasons for her unsmiling face.

Once, she thought her father was going to help her. He was a kind man, a gentle hypochondriac. He would listen. But every conversation that you had with him always turned into a discussion of his imaginary illnesses. He took his blood pressure twice a day and had a graph of its rises and falls on his bedroom wall. He swallowed vitamin pills like sweets and read medical books like other dads read car and computer magazines. Every time he passed a mirror he poked out his tongue to examine it and dragged down the skin below his eyes to inspect his eyeballs. He had read once that yellow eyeballs meant a serious disease. But he'd never had a serious disease, just a succession of coughs and colds and twinges that he treated as if they were fatal.

Flora loved him very much, even though he exasperated her. He was like a big soft friendly kid who needed lots of attention. But one day she had seen how useless it was to expect him to protect her.

They were shadowing her home from school as usual, sometimes calling out but mostly not bothering, talking between themselves. Head down, she scurried in front. When she turned into her street she always hoped they might drop away and let her go. Once or twice, when they had been in a hurry to get home, they had done this. But today they were not in a hurry. They had all the time in the world. And they had stopped talking—they were concentrating on her. This was a bad sign.

'Baby!' her ex-friend started up—she always took the initiative, while the other followed. 'She's always running away, isn't she?' she announced in a loud jeering voice to the other.

'She's pathetic, isn't she?'

'Pathetic,' parroted the other.

As always, Flora pretended not to hear. In any case, they never said anything original—they'd used the same insults a thousand times before. She just closed down her mind and walked on, her face expressionless as a zombie.

The crack of a stone on the wall made her look up sharply. She dropped her head again. It was a long time since they had thrown stones—she must have done something today to irritate them. They didn't hit her with the stones. They aimed, contemptuously, to miss.

But she'd seen something else when she raised her head. She'd seen her father, at the upstairs window of the house, looking down at the grim little scene being played out beneath him. It was the time of day when he took his blood pressure—4.30 precisely.

He must have seen the stone throwing, heard their taunting as they circled, screaming with laughter, round her. The fact that she'd never ever broken into a run helped her retain a shred of personal dignity. Also, they had never made her cry. She didn't cry now, or run. She just walked, her face tight with misery, to their front gate.

Later, her dad said, 'Saw you playing about with your friends out there.' And she would have forgiven him. Except for the fact that she knew, in her heart, that he was quite aware of what was going on. But he was taking his blood pressure. He didn't want to interrupt this ritual. He didn't want to get involved and raise his blood pressure and spoil the smooth line on his graph.

The station clock tower said 11.05. And still Flora stood dithering. 11.10—and Maddy had already left the library but Flora didn't know that. 'If I go down Moravian Street,' she told herself, 'I'll only be a few minutes late. Maybe she'll have waited.'

Anyone watching this scene, unaware of the monumental struggle going on in Flora's mind, would have been baffled. Twice, she raced up the steps by the station—this would take her, via an alleyway, to the top of Moravian Street. Twice she stopped and trailed back down to the beach and stood there, scuffling her feet in the shells, squelching

32

seaweed into green slime. She stuffed her fist into her mouth and chewed her knuckles.

But really, she knew that she was kidding herself, pretending that she had a choice. She knew all along that she wasn't going to take that short cut. Even fear of Maddy's supercilious look couldn't make her brave Moravian Street. The block in her mind was too great.

11.30—it was far too late now. 'She'll have gone now,' Flora reassured herself. 'She'll have gone to interview that man. No point in rushing now.' She felt limp with relief that she didn't have to think about Moravian Street any more. 'Might as well carry on along the beach.'

After all, she had time to kill. She would, she resolved, give Maddy about an hour, then call in at the library, to see if she had gone back there. She didn't know where else to look. The library was their only point of contact. Flora had no idea where Maddy lived—Maddy had not told her.

Flora felt safe out on the shoreline. Everyone was crammed into the town, Christmas shopping. There was no one out here. Glistening mud-flats surrounded and protected her. No danger could come close without her seeing. She ambled along, holding up her face to winter sunshine. She didn't once feel the need to check over her shoulder.

In front of her, a mile or so away, the hulk of the *Raider* rose above the scrubby sandhills. Slowly, killing time, Flora made her way towards it from the south while Maddy, at more or less the same time, was approaching it from the north.

4

A creepy chill of recognition stopped Maddy in her tracks. She hesitated. Then reluctantly, as if against her will, she stumbled down the beach and out on to the mud-flats to get closer to the rotting hulk of the *Arctic Raider*.

The *Raider*, or what was left of her, towered above Maddy. The trawler was a metal ruin. She had been towed down a channel to the breaker's yard. But the channel was dry now. You could, if you didn't mind slithering on stinking mud, walk all the way round her.

Even though she was stripped of her fishing gear and pinned down by metal cables, the *Raider* was still power-ful—majestic as a castle ruin. The low winter sun gilded the corroding metal, laced the mud around her with shadows.

Maddy crept nearer, fascinated despite herself. She had thought that all the trawlers had been scrapped long ago. The *Raider* must be the last trawler in town.

She had been ripped apart so you could look inside her as you peer inside a doll's house. A third of the ship had been amputated. Pipeshafts protruded like severed arteries. Inside were galleries of dark and rusty metal caves.

And it was so quiet. Even the seagulls seemed to avoid this place. The sun shifted and slid into the carcass of the gutted trawler.

Maddy shivered and, despite herself, looked over her shoulder. She felt as if there were ghosts here.

She had seen a film years ago (it had scared her to death—she had hidden behind the sofa with her fingers in her ears) where scattered bones all came together, a skeleton leapt up and chased jerkily after the hero. If you lopped off its skull or bony arm it just reassembled itself. The bits converged as if by magic to make it whole again. Nothing could stop it. She could imagine the *Raider* assembling quietly in the dark, then making its escape from this graveyard—a ghostly hulk sailing out on the tide in a misty dawn to haunt the old fishing grounds. With winches screaming, engines whining at full steam ahead and Laurie, drowned forty years ago, standing on the bridge.

She whirled round, consumed by childhood fears, and almost bumped into someone. Horrified, she shrieked and cringed away. Maddy wasn't given to shrieking—it was too uncool. She got a crazed fast-forward blur of boots, rough coat, large hands, a panicky impression of bulk and height, before she turned and fled in the wrong direction, out on to the mud-flats.

Flora, as she neared the breaker's yard, met the man Maddy had run away from. She shrank inside as he approached along the beach because he looked so threatening. Head down, she hurried by, careful to make no eye contact. But he didn't seem to see her. In a world of his own, his lips working silently, he lumbered past in black seaman's boots and a great grey flapping overcoat. She thought he might be drunk.

She squinted over her shoulder, just to make sure he wasn't turning back. She didn't like the look of him at all. He was big, like a shambling bear, but it was the back of his head that spooked her most. His hair was shaved, a brutal, skinhead cut. But the skin on his skull wasn't tight, like a young man's head. It was baggy, pleated, with stubble crawling in and out of the folds.

She forgot him almost immediately. As she neared the hulk of the *Raider* the sun, already setting, struck full on it so the ship's corrosion seemed like radiant gold and the creek, filling now with water, was on fire.

Maddy was bent double, gasping for breath, with a scorching pain in her side. The shoreline was hazy in the distance: she was a long way out, surrounded by mud-flats and water and sky. But, at first, this didn't bother her—as long as she'd escaped from the man and from the *Arctic Raider*.

She straightened up. The quiet seascape with its fretted sand and oily creeks calmed her. She didn't notice that the tide was surging in.

'What's the matter with you!' she hissed to herself in a voice still fluttery with tension. 'You're falling apart, losing control. Don't be so pathetic!' She took several deep breaths—and felt better.

But now that she had stopped running, Maddy began, gradually, to sink. Under the greasy crust there was black mud, sticky as tar. As her shoes were sucked down into it, clear salt water bubbled up round her ankles.

That was when Flora spotted her. She recognized her straightaway—that long tawny hair and Maddy's distinctive skiing jacket—an expensive one, black with a silver eagle on the back. No one else in town had a coat like that.

She saw Maddy jerk her head up and look round as if she'd only just realized the danger she was in. Flora could see it more clearly than she could. On either side of Maddy, deep fast-flowing creeks, carved into the mud-flats, were racing in a pincer movement to the beach. They would link up and flood the place where Maddy stood. The tide here was notoriously swift and deadly. Many people had been drowned. You looked at it one minute and it was below the horizon—you saw nothing but empty miles of mud and sand. You looked again and it was slopping round your shoes.

Maddy grasped her leg and tugged, trying to drag it loose. It didn't budge, as if her foot was screwed into a vice.

She began to yell. 'Help me! Help!' Her voice was swallowed up by a low rumbling growl. It was the sound of the tide, powering in as if driven by some gigantic engine.

Maddy could see now how the tide was pumping through the channels. How the sluggish creek over to her right was swelling to a river. Even from here she could see it swirling, see waves thrashing on to the mud-flats, leaving scummy trails of foam.

Flora hesitated. She wasn't thinking about the danger she'd be in if she went to help Maddy. She was thinking, What if she doesn't like it, being helped by me? What if she says, 'Piss off. I don't need your help'?

Maddy yelled again, her voice a shrill thread of panic, barely audible.

There was no time left for agonized speculation. Flora began to run.

Maddy tugged again and again at her leg. She was whimpering. But she didn't know it—she couldn't hear her own voice above the growling of the surf. Then, with a sudden *glug*, the mud spewed up her shoe, throwing her wildly off balance.

'It's OK. I've got you! You won't fall!'

Maddy's head whipped round as someone clasped her arm and steadied her. For a second, Flora's face raised nothing but a question mark in her mind . . .

'Come on,' urged Flora, as Maddy's blank expression flooded with recognition, 'before we start sinking. We haven't got much time.'

They didn't speak again. Just staying upright took all their concentration. Their ear-drums were battered with a roaring din. All around, the racing tide made the mud-flat boom as if it was a giant thundering drum. The surface flexed beneath them like a slippery membrane—as queasily unstable as walking on a water-bed. Clinging together for support they floundered back. Sea welled up in their footsteps, pursuing them to shore. At the narrowest point, where the rivers collided, they had to take a desperate running jump to clear the torrent. On the far side, the bank crumbled away like cake beneath their scrabbling hands.

But the mud-flats had given way to sand. They were safe, above the tideline.

Both of them collapsed on to the narrow strip of beach. For some minutes, Flora was too shattered to do anything but hang her head, exhausted, and struggle to control her rattling breath.

Then she noticed dry, crispy seaweed where her hand rested, felt chilly, damp sand beneath her thighs. She scratched her head—her hair was crusted with salt crystals.

And, beside her, Maddy spoke. 'Look at these boots. They're ruined and I only got them yesterday. They cost a fortune, these did.'

All Flora's apprehensions came swooping back. Out on the mud-flats, the place where Maddy had been trapped was ten feet beneath the waves. But it didn't occur to Flora that she may have just saved Maddy's life, or that Maddy owed her anything. She still felt the need to apologize for herself. She felt someone like Maddy would expect it.

'I'm sorry about missing our meeting,' she began awkwardly. 'You know—that meeting at 11 o'clock. I went to see someone—to get some information for our project. I got a little bit. Not much though.'

Flora scanned Maddy's face, watching for her reaction. She expected irritation, even scorn. But found instead a distracted look as if Maddy had forgotten about the library and the history project altogether.

Flora hunted in her pocket for her notebook to prove to Maddy that her excuse was genuine. 'Look.' She fluttered the book under Maddy's nose. 'I made these notes.'

But Maddy's attention wasn't on her—it was somewhere very far away. She didn't even glance at the book. Desperately, Flora said, 'He told me about this ship—the *Arctic Raider*. Look, I've written it down.'

'What?'

Flora cringed—she mistook Maddy's shocked voice for anger. She gabbled, 'I went to see this old man and he told me he worked on the *Arctic Raider* and that the skipper was a bastard and that on Christmas Day this deckie-learner went overboard on their best trip ever.' Throughout this breathless explanation Flora pointed to each of her notes in turn:

1. Arctic Raider
2. Bastard

3. Christmas Day
4. Best Trip Ever

Maddy turned her haunted gaze on Flora. 'Did you
know,' she said, 'that the *Raider* is a very famous ship?'
'Er, no.'
'And do you know where she is now?'
Again, Flora shook her head. If these questions were
Maddy's way of testing her, then she was failing, dismally.
'She's there,' whispered Maddy. And even Flora could
tell that there was dread, not anger, in her voice. 'She's
there, right in front of you.'
If she had been her usual self, there's no doubt that
Maddy would have been checking up and down the
beach—to make sure that none of her friends had witnessed
that undignified rescue, by someone so uncool. But today's
events had thrown her off-balance. She had let her image
slip, badly. It was lucky that the only person there to see was
Flora.
Flora got up from the sand. Picking her way through
twisted metal she went down to the water's edge. She could
just make out the name *ARCTIC RAIDER*. The sunlight had
left the wreck now and it was a sombre gun-metal grey with
grey creek water slopping round it. Cables and pipe casings
snaked out of it. The *Raider* was disabled—just a shell—but
she didn't look broken. She was still dangerous. It was high
tide—dead calm. That eerie hush before the sea churns,
then erupts again into roaring motion.
Then Flora saw that you could get on board the *Raider*.
There was a way into those dark caverns. At the back of the
ship, out of sight of the beach, was a plank stretching from
the mud-flats, over the creek to a yawning hole in the
Raider's hull. She turned and found Maddy by her side,
chewing at a strand of hair. 'We can get on board,' said
Flora.
'What for?' Maddy tried to make her voice sound off-
hand, casual. But she was thinking about Laurie. He was a
wimp—she had established that. But she couldn't help

39

remembering the room of nets and his silky baby hair, glittering in the mesh. It made her shudder, as if someone was walking on her grave. But she wasn't going to spill out her fears to Flora—she planned to be frosty and aloof. Particularly after that rescue, which might make Flora become familiar, as if Maddy owed it to her to be friendly.

No chance! thought Maddy. This partnership is strictly business.

'I think,' Flora was saying, 'I'll just have a look. The *Raider* is the last trawler—the last trawler in town. If we're writing about fishing, we should go on board a trawler, shouldn't we?'

'I don't see why,' said Maddy with an exasperated pout. 'It's only a crappy history project, for Chrissake.'

She thought that Flora would take the hint and not go on board. But Flora took no notice. She was already half-way across the gangplank. This mini-mutiny surprised and peeved Maddy. She'd taken it for granted that Flora would be easy to boss around.

Flora, too, was surprised by her own strength of purpose. She never gave herself credit—she was convinced she was a coward. And it was true that she was afraid most of the time. Afraid of being in school, afraid of walking home, afraid of Moravian Street. Yet underneath that fear was a bedrock of dogged defiance. She would lower her head, cut herself off, and simply survive—tight-lipped, dead-eyed, stone-faced, scared. But still alive inside.

So now, her ears shut to Maddy's scorn, Flora went on board the *Raider*. It wasn't really for their project. She felt a personal curiosity, a powerful attraction. The dark scared her. But dark and lonely places were refuges to Flora. And she was used, after lots of practice, to being scared. It seemed a normal state of mind to her.

As soon as she ducked inside the jagged hole in the *Raider*'s hull, the outside world and Maddy ceased to exist.

She was in chilly half-light, stooping in a tiny metal cave, its walls seamed with rivets. Peeling paint and corroded metal brushed off in her hair. Rainbows shivered in the oil puddles on the floor. Luminous orange water dribbled from the roof. There was a strange metallic taste in the air, like the tainted contents of an old tin can. And, everywhere, rust flowers bloomed—from palest orange to deepest red—as if this was a garden of decay. Corrosion dripped and glistened in the dark.

So near that if she stretched out her hand she could reach it, was another opening that would lead her deeper into the ship. But she stayed where she was. She didn't feel like exploring.

In the gloom, Flora remembered the deckie-learner, that 'poor boy' who'd gone overboard on Christmas Day. Who'd frozen to death in Arctic waters as the *Raider* steamed into the distance. 'We made his life hell,' Mr Walters had told her. And Flora could sense that boy's fear as if it sweated from the walls. She recognized those feelings. And wondered if the boy had ever cowered here. Some of her own bolt-holes were not much different to this. She had no idea what had really happened nearly half a century ago. The Iceman, the crew, Mr Walters: she had no idea what part these people had played in the deckie-learner's story. She didn't even know his name. She only knew his story had a tragic ending.

'Don't be so morbid!' she jeered at herself. 'Just get out of here. There's nothing to see, nothing that's any use for our project. It's just some old wreck, that's all.'

But for a moment she thought she had linked minds across the years with that tormented boy . . .

'Don't be stupid!'

She forced herself to look into the next metal cell.

What she saw there made her dive towards the daylight and wobble down the springy gangplank—back to Maddy and the safety of the shore.

5

'There's someone *living* in there,' were Flora's first breathless words to Maddy. 'I'm not kidding! There's a bed in
there—a camping bed and some blankets and—' Eager to
explain, she grasped Maddy by the sleeve of her expensive
jacket. Irritation flared in Maddy's face—Flora snatched
back her hand as if it had been burned. Confused, she
finished, '—and some food and a torch—'

'It's that man,' interrupted Maddy with lofty conviction.
She paused to brush her sleeve, as if Flora had
contaminated it. And caught sight of a wisp of blond hair
clinging to the glossy black material. Agitated, she plucked
it off and flicked it away. But it curled like a ring around
her finger. She scrubbed her hand on her jeans. Flora
waited, mystified. When Maddy looked again, the hair had
gone.

Less haughty now, she appealed to Flora, 'It must have
been him, mustn't it? You saw him, didn't you? He came
from out of nowhere. But he must have been aboard the
Raider. He's not allowed to do that, is he? I mean, he's a
squatter, isn't he? We should inform the police—'

'Can't think why anybody wants to live in there.' Flora
felt her shoulders scrunch into a shudder. 'He must be
crazy, wanting to live in there.' Among the ghosts, she
thought. But she didn't say that to Maddy.

'Among the ghosts,' said Maddy as if she could read
minds.

'What?'

'You know, that boy that died. That man I went to see this
morning, Mr Pederson—well, he was Laurie's father. But I
didn't even see him. I saw Laurie's mother, Mrs Pederson
and . . .' Maddy hesitated. There was no way she had meant
to favour Flora with any information about her personal

42

anxieties. But so what? she reassured herself. She can't tell anyone. She doesn't know anyone to tell.

'Did you say his name was Laurie?'

'Yes,' nodded Maddy impatiently as if it was an irrelevant detail.

But to Flora it was an intense emotional shock, knowing the name of the boy who, a moment ago, had only his fear to identify him.

'And you've seen his parents?' marvelled Flora. With every second Laurie's bones were taking on more flesh.

But Maddy was already rushing on, words tumbling out, as if her reckless, uncool decision to confide in Flora had broken down other barriers in her mind.

'There was this crazy room, all full of nets—up in the attic. His mum, she made all these nets after Laurie died, sort of to remember him by. And it's dead creepy—it's got all his toys, model aeroplanes, marbles, school reports. Even his baby hair, from his first haircut . . .'

Maddy flashed a threatening glance at Flora, defying her to show the faintest sign of disbelief or scorn.

But Flora's only expression was shocked fascination, like a kid watching a horror video. Gratified, Maddy plunged on: 'And his mother was a real head-case. Going on about him as if he was still alive, about how he loved the *Arctic Raider*, how he loved the sea and how everybody loved him. It was enough to make you sick! If you ask me, he was dead soft, a real mother's boy. He sounded like a wimp in this journal thing he wrote in—'

'Are you sure,' said Flora, struggling to cope with the bizarre vision Maddy's words revealed to her, 'are you sure we're talking about the same boy? The same boy that Mr Walters was telling me about?'

Flora checked the facts she knew off on her fingers, one by one. 'He was the deckie-learner on the *Raider*. Right? Sixteen years old. And he went overboard on Christmas Day on the *Raider*'s best trip ever? Right? And the skipper, who they called the Iceman, was a real bastard?'

'I don't know.' Maddy shook her head. 'I don't know

43

anything about the skipper. Mrs Pederson never said about him. She probably would have done if I'd stayed any longer. But I wasn't going to hang around there. I was off the first chance I got!'

'Some things don't add up,' murmured Flora, deep in thought.

'Oh, come on, it's got to be the same boy. That's obvious. Only he never went overboard on Christmas Day. I'm sure about that because his mother said he had his Christmas dinner. She said he saw the New Year in.' Maddy scowled, searching in her memory. 'I know. She said it was January sometime, a day before the *Raider* got home—'

'Well, Mr Walters never said that. He said Christmas Day definitely. I wrote that down.'

Flora spoke with greater urgency as more and more of Mr Walters' words unravelled from her memory. 'And he said this boy went overboard in Arctic waters. I remember that because he said he would have froze to death in two minutes. And he didn't tell me all this stuff about everybody liking him. He said the crew made his life hell. He even said that when he went overboard the *Raider* never went back for him and nobody even cared.'

'Look, I don't know,' protested Maddy, angry at being contradicted. 'I mean, I never knew anything about him before this morning! He was dead boring anyway. But I'm the one who saw his mother. You didn't. And his own mother should know when he died, shouldn't she? Shouldn't she?'

Flora gave a grudging nod.

'Well, that proves it, then,' said Maddy, slightly appeased now it seemed that Flora had backed down. 'The old guy that you saw must have got things wrong. Was he a bit senile or something?'

Flora shrugged her shoulders.

'I thought so,' cried Maddy. But she resented the doubtful look that still remained on Flora's face.

'I can't understand it,' muttered Flora. 'They can't both be right.'

'For Heaven's sake. I've told you, his mother's right—about the dates and everything. I mean, she should know about her own son, shouldn't she? Look, if you don't believe me, let's go back and see his mother and ask her.'

Maddy could have bitten her tongue off. She hadn't meant to say that. She couldn't believe that she felt she had something to prove to this girl, who was so far outside the in-group that she might have been on the rim of the world.

'Cheek!' she blustered to herself, to cover her fear at having foolishly volunteered to go back to that creepy household. 'She doesn't know anything about it. I'm the one who saw his mother. I read his diary. I saw his photos.' She had forgotten about that. 'I saw Laurie's photo,' she informed Flora smugly. 'I know what he looks like.'

'His photo? Did you really see his photo?' Flora, anxious for more information, ran to keep up with Maddy. Behind them, the *Raider* squatted in the mud and kept her secrets to herself.

'Yes,' announced Maddy, keeping her voice cool. 'There were loads of photos of him, hung among those nets. In that room I told you about. There was everything about him in that room.'

'Do you think that I could see that room?'

Flora's voice had too much pleading in it. Maddy knew that she was back in charge. She sucked her breath in in a doubtful hiss. 'Well, I don't know,' she teased, with that familiar twinge of horror at her own nastiness. 'Mrs Pederson's got a bad heart. Wouldn't surprise me if she dropped dead at any minute. Poor old cow might be dead now. Then you'd never get in to see those photos, would you?'

'But you only saw her a couple of hours ago,' protested Flora. 'She can't have dropped dead since then.'

Maddy shrugged. 'Shouldn't be surprised . . . But anyway, she doesn't know who you are, does she? I mean, my interview was all arranged. My parents fixed it up for me.' Mentioning her parents made Maddy remember that

45

they were two hundred miles away. She bet that there'd be loads of messages on the answerphone—one for every service station they'd stopped at. She smiled, in fond exasperation.

They were walking past the docks now, through scrubby patches of wasteland. Jetties, algal-green, marched out through mud to nowhere. Over to their left was the library, the town centre office blocks, and the busy shopping malls. Here the dockland was quietly decaying away.

Most of the warehouses were derelict. One or two were still in use. They were fenced-in like prison camps. Behind the barbed wire forklift trucks snarled about in the loading yards.

Maddy strode in front. Flora trotted behind, thinking about Laurie.

Everyone—Maddy, his mother, Mr Walters—seemed to have a different story to tell about Laurie. But she wanted to hear Laurie's own voice. She wanted to read that journal in the room of nets, find out who he really was. Most of all she wanted to know the truth about his death.

It surprised her that she cared this much about someone who was ancient history, who'd been lost at sea forty years ago. But ever since she'd been on the *Raider*, Flora had felt a peculiar solidarity with Laurie. As if his misery, his terror, had never died but reached out to her across the years. And she'd made a sudden decision. She'd decided that Laurie needed a protector, someone who could understand him. Maddy, who had always been protected, couldn't understand him. And if Laurie's mother was anything like her own, she didn't understand him either. Only she, Flora, could rescue him from the confusion of the past. She would be Laurie's champion. She wanted to stand up for him, give him an identity, a voice, because nobody stood up for her when, so often over these past years, she'd felt as trembly and insubstantial as the shadows on the wall.

You and me against the world, Laurie, she thought. She felt tears pricking in her eyes and rubbed them away, embarrassed.

46

She knew that she was being over-emotional. But, for once, she didn't care. It was a long time since she'd allowed herself to feel any self-pity for her own situation. Laurie would understand.

And she knew perfectly well that you can hardly protect someone who's already dead. All the same, it gave her a buzz of confidence to think that she was fighting on Laurie's behalf. She wouldn't give up easily. She could be stubborn as hell.

With her face set in a ferocious, tearful scowl, Flora trudged after Maddy's elegant figure.

It didn't surprise her at all that Laurie's mother insisted that he was wonderfully happy. If anyone had asked her mother about her, the answer would have been, 'Oh, Flora? She's all right. Getting on well at school. A bit quiet—but no trouble at all. You hardly know she's there.'

'I'll find out, Laurie,' whispered Flora. 'They can't hide anything from me.'

This was getting weird, making promises to a dead boy. Usually Flora didn't allow herself such imaginative indulgences. She had learned that it was better not to. She tried to snap back to reality, forcing herself to focus on the cracks in the pavement, the skin of frost already re-forming, the sign that she had just passed that said: MORAVIAN STREET . . .

Panic beat inside her brain like wings.

She whirled round, frantic to get her bearings. Behind her was a narrow strip of pale tarmac, two rows of dull houses. That splash of crimson and dark green was a Christmas garland on a door. Like a dreamer roughly shaken awake, she gawped about her. She couldn't understand what was going on. As if she'd woken up on the safe side of a treacherous canyon without knowing how she'd crossed it.

'Come on,' yelled Maddy. 'What are you standing there for? You're the one that wanted to go to this place, aren't you? You're the one that made all the fuss about this Laurie. Don't you want to go now?' asked Maddy hopefully. The nearer they got to Mrs Pederson's house, the more scared and vulnerable she felt.

But Flora nodded dumbly.

'Come on, then!' barked Maddy. She hardly ever did things that she didn't want to. She never did things that upset her. She couldn't understand how she'd got herself into this mess.

Flora stumbled after her. Her brain couldn't cope with what had just happened. It was too momentous. It blew wide open all the restrictions that controlled her life.

So she filed away the amazing, alarming knowledge that she'd just walked through Moravian Street—and survived. She would think about it later. She was too busy to think about it now.

6

Mrs Pederson lived in a quiet, leafy avenue where, from one week to the next, nothing ever happened.

But today was different. The avenue was buzzing. Maddy and Flora walked straight into a scene from a television soap. An ambulance was slewed on to the pavement, back door flung wide, blue light whirling.

A knot of onlookers stared—but kept a polite distance. It was that kind of neighbourhood.

Then, the deep shrubbery in front of Mrs Pederson's house rustled and spat out paramedics, a stretchered body, other people running after. Ten seconds and the street was clear again: the stretcher slotted in, Mr Pederson's lean stooping figure hustled after it, doors secured, an engine *vrooming* into life.

The whining siren was two streets away before anyone realized the show was over. The watchers lingered, half-expecting more thrills to follow. But there was nothing left to see.

'They were fifteen minutes trying to revive her,' said one, spinning out the drama.

'That was just to make him feel better. They say that she was dead before she hit the floor . . .'

But their hearts weren't in it. No one had known much about the Pedersons. They kept themselves to themselves. In the end, the watchers drifted back home, feeling vaguely cheated.

Maddy and Flora, creeping up in time to hear these comments, were left alone. The avenue's brief skirmish with excitement was over. All tidied away, back to normal.

Sick with disbelief, Maddy turned to Flora. 'Did you see that?' she said, as if the incident had been a hologram, projected on the winter afternoon.

49

She tried to swallow but her throat seemed locked. She was thinking about that malicious prophecy made, so casually, just half an hour ago. About the time that Mrs Pederson's heart stopped beating.

It was a joke, she wailed, inside her mind. I didn't mean it. I didn't *really* want her to drop dead. What did she have to go and do that for?

Maddy shivered, her face grim, appalled. Any mention of death spooked her anyway. She had never personally crossed paths with death—never been to a funeral. All her grandparents were still alive. Yet here, she and death had met face-to-face. And he was shaking his bones at her.

She wasn't used to facing things on her own. She hadn't been packed in cotton wool exactly, but her parents were fixers, pushy and persuasive people who changed things for Maddy's benefit. If anything went wrong, they zoomed in like International Rescue and got her out of trouble. Now Maddy felt as if a monster had been loosed, something with teeth and claws, too fearsome for her to cope with. But International Rescue were in a Volvo 200 miles down the motorway. The only person here was Flora.

'It's all my fault,' muttered Maddy.

'What did you just say?' asked Flora, over her shoulder. She had been looking at the house: blank dead windows, grey stone, dark-green laurel.

'It's all my fault,' repeated Maddy, peeved that Flora wasn't paying more attention. 'I said about her dying—and she did.'

'Don't be stupid,' said Flora, turning back to the house. 'It's got nothing to do with you.'

She was too fired up to bother about Maddy. Being Laurie's champion had made her single-minded. And besides, Maddy was probably posing anyway. Flora had noticed that Maddy and her friends did a lot of posing.

Maddy pouted. 'That's easy for you to say.'

But she was genuinely hurt, confused. She had taken it for granted that Flora would be sympathetic. As if someone with so little going for her couldn't afford not to be.

'Where are you going now?'

'I'm just having a little look,' replied Flora, 'round the back of the house.'

'You can't do that,' said Maddy, scandalized. 'Someone might see you. I mean, it's private property. You're trespassing. You can't—'

But Flora had already slipped away. Maddy, left alone in the road, agonized over her next move. She felt sorry for herself, cast adrift, desolate. She wasn't used to such neglect.

It was in her mind to go home, forget about today, run a foamy bath, put on a CD, pop one of the frozen meals her mother had left her into the microwave . . .

But what if, when she'd done all that, and it was growing late and dark, Mrs Pederson, freshly-dead, with her wooden braiding needle rattling in her apron pocket, came looking for revenge?

'Don't be stupid!' she snapped at herself, trying to imitate Flora's dismissive tones. 'You've been getting too many chillers from the video shop!'

But her voice was shaking.

She hesitated. Then ran down the path to find Flora.

'Look,' Flora whispered to her, 'they've left the back door unlocked.' Her face radiated eager determination.

Maddy shrank back. 'We can't go in there! Someone might see us. Think we're stealing something.'

'I just want to look,' explained Flora, soothingly. 'Just take a look at this room of nets. I'll only be a minute. You can stay here if you want to. You can be on guard.'

Maddy gnawed at her lip. 'No, no. I'll come. You'll never find it on your own. But we'll have to be quick. In case someone comes.'

Ever since this morning Maddy's mind had been buzzing like a fly around Mrs Pederson, Laurie, the room of nets. She'd been unable to forget them. Now, it seemed, she'd passed the same obsession on to Flora. Maddy's whole being revolted at the thought of climbing those dark stairs again. But she dared not stay outside. What if someone came? What if Mrs Pederson, with her wooden braiding needle . . . ?

'Jesus!' she growled at herself. 'What's happening to you?'

With a desperate effort she screwed the lid down on her panic. Her face a tight, careful mask of self-control, she followed Flora into the house.

At first they lost their way. Knobbly furniture jabbed them, crowded them in corners. Doors lured them into cupboards.

'No!' Flora's voice was urgent, excited. 'Don't turn on the light. They'll know there's someone in here!'

Obediently Maddy drew her hand back from the switch.

But suddenly her mind rebelled. What the hell am I doing here? she thought, crossly. Taking orders from someone like her? Creeping round this dump in the dark? It's ridiculous!

Her indignation made her feel a lot better.

'Look,' she said, elbowing Flora out of the way. 'Here are the stairs. We go up to the top. Right? Then one quick look—and we're gone. Right?'

'Right.'

Maddy swept upwards—her fear, for the moment, edged out by her relief at being in charge again.

'Just a quick look. OK?'

She didn't look back. She just assumed that Flora would keep up. But on the second landing Flora lost sight of her and took a wrong turn in the rabbit warren corridors.

Even the cramped top flight, fitting her shoulders like a coffin, didn't jar Maddy's newly-recovered confidence. She trampled on those sinister crimson swirls without a qualm.

'Only a minute, mind,' said Maddy, flinging instructions back into the empty darkness. 'And then we're out of here. You do understand that, don't you? I mean I'm not prepared to hang around any longer—'

The attic door was open, very slightly, with just a slit between the door and the frame. With deliberate contempt for Flora's warning, Maddy thrust her arm into the gap, groping around for a light switch. She's not going to tell me what to do, she was thinking. I'll turn a light on if I want to.

The room of nets got her.

Immediately, her hand was caught, tangled up. She couldn't pull it back.

'Shit.' She tugged indignantly. But she was stuck, helpless, one arm jammed up to the shoulder inside the room and her face flattened against the door, as if she was eavesdropping.

'Shit! Shit!' Panicky thoughts fizzed through her mind like electric currents down a wire.

It was the nightmare situation—the childhood terror. Reaching under the bed for a lost toy. Sliding her arm in up to the shoulder. And something, whatever bogyman it is that lurks in the dark under beds, grabs her. Makes her wriggle and shriek while he chomps her arm like a chicken drumstick. Right down to gleaming bone . . .

'Stay cool. You're just caught in a net, that's all. Just stay cool.' But her face was burning hot.

She yanked hard, twisting her arm to drag it loose. But this time she felt, no mistake, meshes squeeze her wrist, chafing it with rough twine. She struggled, her brow damp with sweat. But the more she pulled, the more, behind the door, the rope noose tightened. And every nerve in her lost arm quivered, anticipating that first bite.

'This is really stupid.' Tears of frustration stung her eyes. 'Flora! Flora!' Her voice echoed pitifully down the stair well.

She rested, slumped against the door. Calmer, she began to feel round, experimentally, with her trapped hand, working out how to escape. She began wriggling her fingers free.

Footsteps! Inside the room, her fevered brain shrieked at her. They're inside the room.

With vicious energy, she hurled herself away from the door, yelping as her arm wrenched—but unscrewed itself anti-clockwise to release the pressure and let her go.

53

She stumbled to her knees among the whirls, scrolls, and hideous scarlet flowers on the carpet. Behind her, the door of the room of nets closed silently against her. There were red bracelets eaten into her bare wrist . . .

Maddy lunged for the stairs. Shoving Flora out of the way she crashed downwards, three at a time.

'Sorry,' Flora panted. 'I got lost. I heard you shouting out. I heard . . .' Her voice trailed into bewildered silence.

Her first impulse was to follow Maddy down. But she hesitated. She was scared—but that was nothing new. The wooden doorknob, polished smooth with handling, responded to the slightest turn of her wrist. She pushed it and walked into the attic.

7

Out to sea, a fiery sun dangled over chilly grey water. Its dying glow smouldered in the room of nets. So, when Flora opened the door, the maze seemed, for a few seconds only, to be pulsing in neon red, all lit up, just for her.

She wandered, bewitched, among the poor remains of Laurie's childhood. As she pushed through, too awestruck to be scared, the nets began to make their jungle sounds: rustling, tinkling, soft scratching, as if they were talking to her.

'Beautiful,' murmured Flora. 'Beautiful.' She gazed upwards, entranced by the billowing nets that swooped above her head.

It was a work of art; Mrs Pederson's secret passion.

Flora peered at photos. She thought Laurie was handsome. She liked his blond, wavy hair and charming grin.

She jingled glass marbles, unfolded brittle school reports and read them. And every find put yet more flesh on Laurie's bones. Until there were no more bones left and Laurie moved around, alive and breathing in her mind.

As she walked, she felt along the walls with her hands to find the places where the mesh yielded and parted to let her through. She was deeper now in the room of nets than Maddy had been. Seeing things that Maddy hadn't seen. Laurie's christening shawl was spread across the net like a big lacy butterfly. She found his cricket bat, his Latin textbook . . .

In her hand, Flora clutched Laurie's 'Seafarer's Journal' —the book Maddy had told her about. She had loosed it from the mesh, meaning to pause to read it. But every time she lifted up a veil, pushed on a little deeper, she glimpsed vivid blue, now here, now there, like an exotic bird flashing through the nets. It drew her on. But it was only when she'd reached journey's end, the far wall of the attic, that she discovered what it was.

'Laurie!' murmured Flora. 'For God's sake! You didn't wear *that*, did you?'

She had walked through the maze feeling solemn, close to tears sometimes. But now, that choked-back emotion exploded in a fit of laughter. It broke the tension. And it finally made Laurie human to her.

She shook her head. 'I've got to tell you, Laurie, that it's really, really terrible.'

She could imagine what the style warriors in Maddy's crowd would have said about Laurie's best suit. It was an amazing suit. Highly fashionable then but only fit to be a clown's suit now. Sky blue, it was, with a pleated jacket, black velvet lapels, half-moon pockets, and impossibly wide trousers.

Flora didn't know it but this suit was Laurie's proudest possession. And he had never seen it. He'd ordered it, his first suit, before he set out on the *Raider* but he'd never gone back to collect it. Those twenty-four inch trousers were the widest you could get. And he'd had the choice of sky blue or pillar box red. He chose the blue.

Flora wiped her eyes, still grinning. Maybe Laurie, with his fresh boy's face and Latin textbook, thought a suit like this would give him street cred. Poor kid, thought Flora. Poor stupid kid. But her smile was one of understanding. She had no style either. All the excruciating fashion mistakes she'd ever made fast-forwarded through her brain. There were a lot of them. That Lycra bodysuit! Those pink leggings! She cringed when she thought about them.

It was as if she was opening her mind to Laurie, sharing these personal embarrassments. As if Laurie would understand.

She was still absorbed in this one-way conversation when, three flights below her, the back door slammed.

And she remembered she had no right at all to be here.

Whirling round, she dived into the maze. It had grown dark and now she had to grope her way back, feeling along the walls for the gaps. Her hands sketched over scratchy twine, fluttering papers, glossy photos, clicking braiding needles. She yanked the door open. And fled.

Outside the kitchen door there was no sign of Maddy. Flora didn't use the front gate but hurried through the garden, scrambled over the back wall and legged it, still grasping Laurie's Seafarer's Journal.

There was plenty of light to guide her—Mr Pederson's workshop still blazed out through the dusk. Flora didn't stop to glance inside. If she had done, she would have seen models of the *Arctic Raider*, dozens of them, arranged along the shelves. On the workbench, among the woodshavings, was a pile of cut-out shapes. They would be *Arctic Raiders* too, when they were glued together.

That evening, at home alone, Maddy put on all the lights. There were three televisions in the house and every one of them was blaring out on a different channel. She couldn't stop roaming round, rattling the doors to make sure she'd locked them.

At six o'clock her parents phoned.

'Have you made yourself something to eat?'

'No, no, not yet. I only just got in.'

'Did you see Mr Pederson this morning? Was he any help?'

'Er . . . er . . . yes, it was OK.'

'What did you say? I can hardly hear you. This must be a bad line.'

'I said, I did everything I was supposed to do.'

'And you're all right?'

'Yes.'

'Are you sure?'

'Yes, yes,' said Maddy irritably. 'Stop worrying.'

'OK, then, but if you need anything—'

'I know, I know, just go next door to Mrs Simpson.'

'That's right. But we'll be back tomorrow night. About seven o'clock.'

'Bye, then.'

'Bye. Don't forget to switch the security system on when you go to bed.'

'Bye.'

Click. Buzz. They'd rung off.

For ten minutes Maddy sat and chewed her nails with the house lit up like a Christmas tree around her and sound jabbering, cackling, booming from almost every room.

Abruptly, as if she'd reached a decision, she snatched up the telephone directory and flicked through it. She trailed her finger down the page, moving her lips with the names. At one name she stopped. Then picked up the phone and punched in the number.

'Hi, this is Maddy.'

'Oh, hello.' It was Flora's voice, so close that Maddy jumped. The voice sounded wary.

'Er . . .' Maddy was nervous. It was unlike her to be lost for words but for once she couldn't bring herself to ask for what she wanted. She tried for a casual, off-hand approach but ended up sounding petulant and demanding. 'You coming round here tonight, then?' she asked. She made no mention at all of Mrs Pederson's death, or her flight from the room of nets. It was as if those things had never happened.

'What *me*? Come round to *your* house?' Flora's amazement came blasting down the line so raw and undisguised that Maddy was embarrassed.

'Why not?' said Maddy, as if she didn't much care one way or the other. But all the time she was eyeing that deep trench of shadows behind the sofa, thinking, Is that something, crouching there?

She wrenched her attention back to Flora, sounding dubious on the other end of the line. 'Well . . . I don't know if I can.'

Despite her jittery state of mind, Maddy felt a spurt of anger at Flora's reluctance. You'd think, thought Maddy,

that she'd jump at the chance! Under normal circumstances, inviting Flora to sleep over was as wildly
improbable as wearing last year's fashions to a party.

'Please yourself. But I was thinking we could do some
work on the project. You might as well stay the night.
There's plenty of spare beds. My mum and dad are away
until tomorrow.'

'I'll ask my mum.'

While she waited for the answer, Maddy felt her mouth
go dry, saw her knuckles whiten on the telephone receiver.

'I'll come then,' said Flora.

'Great,' whispered Maddy, weak with relief.

'What did you say?'

'I said, get round here any time. Soon as you can.'

'My dad says he'll run me round.' Flora was wondering
whether any of Maddy's friends would be there. She felt hot
with distress at the thought of them sniggering at her
snuggly pyjamas. Or her pink fluffy slippers shaped like
pigs.

'See you then.'

'Wait, wait. You haven't told me where you live . . .'

When Flora arrived, clutching Laurie's Seafarer's Journal
and her history project file, she feared the worst. For every
window throbbed with light, as if Maddy's house was
jumping with people.

'Nice here,' her dad remarked as they turned into
Maddy's street. 'Didn't know you had any friends here.'

'I don't.'

Flora spied through the bubbly window panes into the
glare of a dazzling white kitchen. But all she saw was
Maddy, looking bleak and stranded, sitting alone in the
middle of it.

Inside, Flora perched on the edge of a sofa, juggling her
hot mug of coffee, not daring to rest it on the dark wood
coffee table.

'Oh, just put it anywhere,' said Maddy.

But as soon as she began to talk about Laurie she forgot her unease. 'Look,' she told Maddy, 'I've got Laurie's Seafarer's Journal.'

'You stole it?' Disapproval and admiration mingled in Maddy's voice.

'Well, I didn't mean to. I meant to read it there. But I heard a noise and . . .' Flora shrugged. 'I just ran off with it still in my hands.' But even as she was making this excuse she realized that, if she'd thought about it, she would have taken the journal anyway.

'Have you read it?' asked Maddy, without much interest.

'I've read the first bit. That he wrote on December 13th the night before he sailed on the *Raider*.'

'Well, there isn't any more. He only wrote in it once. Doesn't sound like he's 16 does he? Sounds really immature. Sounds like a 5 year old or something, a baby or something.'

Maddy shouldn't have said that—she couldn't help glancing down at her sleeve, looking for golden curls. She couldn't help recalling Mrs Pederson's voice: 'But you haven't seen his baby shoes yet!'

Today's events haunted Maddy. The nets, the *Raider*, the mud, the man in the grey coat, and worst of all, Mrs Pederson's shocking death: there was so much that was inexplicable, terrifying. Maddy wasn't used to feeling so vulnerable and afraid. She had seen death loads of times, crises of all kinds, powerful emotion—on a television screen. But it hadn't really touched her personally. Things did make her unhappy and, sometimes, she made big dramas out of her distress. But the surface of her life was only ruffled. She soon bounced back.

But now there was no one here to cushion her against life's darker side. No protection—she had to face things on her own. She felt a sickening insecurity, as if normal life was breaking up beneath her feet. And she was slipping into swirling depths below.

No one here to protect her—unless, of course, you counted Flora. But Maddy still resented holding out her hand to someone she would otherwise have ignored or patronized.

Patronizing Laurie made her feel a lot better. As if she was on safe ground again, in familiar territory. 'Yeah,' she shook her head in mock sorrow, 'that poor kid had a lot to learn, didn't he?'

'Wait a minute!' Flora looked up from the journal. Her hands were trembling. 'I've found another entry! In the middle of the book! Christmas Eve, it's dated. The day before he died.'

'He died,' said Maddy sharply, 'in January. I told you that before. His mother said so.'

But Flora wasn't listening. She was trying to decipher Laurie's writing. There were only a few words, scribbled very faintly, in capitals, diagonally across two pages.

'I can hardly read it. No wonder I missed it before.'

'I don't want to hear him,' snapped Maddy, trying to keep the panic out of her voice. She had to fight an impulse to clamp her hands over her ears, just as she did when she was little and there were monsters on the television. 'I don't want to hear anything about him. He's really boring. He won't have anything interesting to say.'

But it was too late. 'Christmas Eve 1952,' Flora read out. 'PLEASE GOD SOMEBODY HELP ME.'

8

Maddy, rumpled and pouchy-eyed, dressed in a baggy nightshirt, opened the door on to a glittering morning. Shivering, she grabbed the milk from the step and dived indoors again.

She shuffled, bare-footed, to the kitchen.

'Hello,' said Flora brightly. 'There's some coffee in the pot.'

Flora had spent the night in Maddy's brother's bedroom, in a bed spiky with Lego and gritty with biscuit crumbs. She had hardly slept. Most of the time she had spent awake staring through the gap in Postman Pat curtains. There was a ring of violet phosphorescence round the moon. Half in a trance she had gazed and gazed at it, wondering how to reach the truth about Laurie.

Maddy grunted something inaudible, dragged her hair out of her eyes, slopped coffee in her mug. She was grouchy in the mornings. But at least the horrors of last night were fast dissolving in this clear winter daylight.

It hadn't been a good night for Maddy either. Her sleep had swarmed with dead people and rotting hulks. And she had woken up fighting for her life in damp twisted sheets, thinking she was trapped in mud or nets.

She groped for the radio and switched it on. A choirboy was trilling 'Away in a Manger'. Maddy groaned, jabbed the 'Off' button and terminated him.

She forced her eyes fully open and looked at Flora for the first time. She expected to regret inviting her. But, oddly enough, it was comforting to see her sitting there. Although Maddy couldn't resist a quick private snicker at that cuddly sleeping suit that made her look like a giant pink teddy bear. Maddy wouldn't be seen dead in an outfit like that.

Underneath Flora's hand, which rested on the kitchen table, was Laurie's Seafarer's Journal. Maddy gave the notebook a furtive, sidelong glance, as if she was afraid of it. She didn't want to talk about Laurie any more, or Mrs Pederson or the *Arctic Raider*. She wanted to lay those ghosts to rest, not resurrect them.

'I've got tons of Christmas shopping to do today,' she announced, flopping into a chair at the kitchen table. Thoughts of the mall, a tinselly Christmas Wonderland, cheered her up no end. She felt like spending lots of money.

'Do you have a real Christmas tree?' she asked Flora. 'Or one of those horrid artificial ones?'

Flora raised her hand from the journal so Maddy could see those blue wavy letters that she'd thought so childish.

'We're going to the Fishing Museum this morning,' said Flora, looking directly into Maddy's eyes. Despite herself, Maddy flinched from that gaze. Before they were partnered for this project, Maddy hadn't given a thought to what Flora was like. She saw her in class every day. But she looked through her, to smile at someone more important, as if Flora was transparent as a sheet of glass. If you had pushed her, Maddy might have managed to describe Flora in negative ways: not funny, not pretty, not one of us. But there was nothing negative about that defiant expression that was challenging her now, across the table.

Maddy disguised her dismay with a snort of mocking laughter. 'Come on! You must be joking! I wouldn't be seen dead anywhere near that dump. Nobody ever goes there.'

'We've got to,' said Flora, as if they had no choice. 'It's the only place I can think of where we might find out about Laurie. They've got records there, newspaper articles, photos, stuff like that. We can't go back to Mr Pederson, not after his wife's just died. And Mr Walters just rambles on—you can hardly understand him. So where else is there?'

Maddy shrugged. She didn't want to get involved with Laurie's story. And she hated being told what to do, especially by Flora. 'What's so important about this

Laurie?' she said viciously. 'I mean, we're supposed to be doing a project here, aren't we? What's it matter whether some stupid kid fell overboard on Christmas Day or a week later? Who could care less? I mean, why do you care? Anybody would think you fancied him or something! Anyone would think you were in love with him. You do know he's dead, don't you? That he's just a pile of bones?'

It gave her a sick twinge of guilt to see Flora blush and stammer: ''Course I know that!' But she couldn't help rushing on. 'He was a wimp anyway,' she declared. 'Not worth bothering about.'

The kitchen chair clattered to the ground as Flora, in her pink teddy bear suit, lunged across the table. Maddy jerked back, already wincing at the blow: 'I w-w-was only joking!'

But Flora didn't hit her. Instead she yelled, eyes blazing, 'Just who the hell do you think you are! You haven't got a clue, have you? You haven't got a clue what it was like for Laurie on the *Raider*? Hiding all the time, scared to death, no one to protect him. They made his life hell, that's what Mr Walters said.'

Maddy circled the table.

'Well, what do you know about that, eh?' raged Flora, stabbing a trembling accusing finger at Maddy's face. 'What could you possibly know about that?'

It was on the tip of Maddy's tongue to jeer, 'So what do *you* know about it, then?' But she didn't dare. She was, for once, tongue-tied, astonished at the violence, the savage resentment in Flora's words. Who'd have guessed that Flora could go beserk like that? Maddy giggled, just to break the tension.

But Flora had already sunk back in her chair, shocked by her own venom. Years of having to run, hide, lock up her emotions, be Stone Face, had left their mark. Bitterness grew deep inside her. Bitterness against her tormentors and against people like Maddy who led charmed lives. Sometimes it surfaced. 'I could kill them. I could kill them all!' she would rave in the privacy of her bedroom. But mostly, scared by the power of her hatred, she kept it chained and buried. She blamed herself, she endured in stony silence—anything but let that hatred loose.

Now Maddy was reeling from its full force. And Maddy's response balanced on a knife edge. She was tempted to be outraged, make a scene, throw Flora out of the house.

But when she saw Flora slumped in her pink furry outfit, Maddy surprised herself by saying, 'Well, all right, then. If you're going to get so worked up about it, we'll go, then.'

It wasn't only sympathy for Flora that made Maddy so obliging. Her other reason was the thought, niggling away in the back of her mind, that this Laurie business wasn't going to go away, just because she wanted it to. That, somehow, the ghost of Mrs Pederson wouldn't be laid until the mystery of Laurie's death had been cleared up. Common sense told her this notion was crazy. But, all the same, she couldn't help believing it.

'We'll go, then,' repeated Maddy.

Flora didn't even look up. But she didn't feel angry any more. She felt weak but relaxed, as if she'd just stepped out of a hot bath.

Maddy waited, expecting an apology. But Flora didn't apologize, or look grateful. She just said, 'Right, that's settled then. I'll go and get dressed.'

Maddy gaped, open-mouthed, after her.

Then she shrugged—and slouched over to slot two pieces of bread into the toaster.

'Flora! Do you want smooth or crunchy peanut butter on your toast?' she yelled up the stairs.

The Fishing Museum, forgotten by almost everyone in town, was tucked away on the docks among the vast warehouses and derelict Victorian buildings.

'Are you sure it's still open?' said Maddy. 'I've never met anyone who's been there.'

But Flora was too choked with tension to reply. For they were walking down Moravian Street. And this time, she was super-alert to what was going on. Her nerves twitched at every flick of the curtains, every shadowy movement deep inside dark rooms. Her senses had never been so keen— jumpy as any hunted creature's.

She'd known, two streets away, which route they were going to take. And her mind had cringed in protest: 'I'm not going down there!' But Moravian Street was the natural short cut to the beach and docks. And, in the end, she couldn't find a single, sensible excuse for avoiding it.

No one could have guessed, from Flora's steely face, what desperate, reckless schemes were writhing in her head as they approached Moravian Street.

Pretend to be ill, Flora's brain was yammering at her. Faint! Fall down! Say you've bust your leg.

It was no good. She was a lousy actress. And too proud to play the fool in front of Maddy. So with zombie eyes and strange robotic movements as if her limbs were radio controlled, she tottered into Moravian Street. While the muscles that drove her onwards ached to run in the opposite direction.

It was her worst nightmare. *They* were there, both of them, lounging against a garden wall. At the first sight of Flora they sprang up, excited, as if they couldn't believe their luck. They had her trapped, on their territory—it was a chance in a million. And they weren't going to waste it. One of them, the leader, changed her incredulous expression to a slow smile. She turned to the other, raised her eyebrows and jerked her thumb in Flora's direction. They both laughed. It had been a really boring day—until now.

Then, a miracle happened.

Maddy, who'd lagged behind to re-tie the laces of her trainers, jogged up to join Flora. To Flora's confusion, she linked arms, pulled Flora close to her as if they were the best of friends.

And the two, who were already closing in, shrank back. Shrivelled up the garden path, like slugs drenched with salt.

What's going on? thought Flora, bewildered.

It was amazing—as if she had a magic talisman to ward

off evil. Thwarted, her persecutors glowered from the safety of the garden, kept off by Maddy's presence.

Maddy knew she was protecting Flora, but she gave no sign of it. She looked straight through the two girls from her class as if they were invisible. And swept by, haughty and confident as always. 'Vicious little cows,' she hissed under her breath, too softly for Flora to hear.

She propelled Flora to the end of Moravian Street. Then, when they had turned the corner, let go of her arm.

And suddenly, Flora felt bitter laughter bursting inside her like pain. Years and years of scurrying round back streets and alleys—and all it took to intimidate them was someone like Maddy, strolling in apparent friendship beside her. Maddy thought those two were nothing—hardly worth her contempt. Yet, until this precise moment, they had controlled Flora's life so completely that she scarcely made a move without thinking about them first. Flora allowed herself a grim chuckle at the craziness of it all.

'What's so funny?' Maddy asked her.

'Nothing's funny. Nothing at all. Look, thanks for what you did back there.'

Sometimes Maddy could be stunningly thoughtless. But then she'd surprise you with an act so generous and gracious that your heart warmed to her. She did that now. She opened her eyes wide, shrugged, put on her most innocent expression. 'No need to thank me. What did I do? I didn't do anything at all.'

And they didn't speak about it again.

9

Maddy and Flora crossed the disused railway line. Just round the corner was the breaker's yard where the *Raider* was quietly corroding in mud.

But they weren't going in that direction.

'Where is this Fishing Museum?' complained Maddy. 'Are you sure it exists?'

'' 'Course it exists.' Flora could dimly recall going there, years ago, on a school trip. There'd been lots of models of ships in dusty glass cases.

They walked past the first dock, once jammed with ships, now empty and still as a swimming pool after closing time. Except that its water was rainbow-slicked with oil spillage and littered with seagulls' feathers.

Apart from themselves, and an optimistic angler way out on a jetty, there was nobody about.

'I think,' said Flora, scowling with the effort of remembering, 'I think it's just past the Royal Dock.'

To their surprise, there was one lonely boat in the Royal Dock. It was a little inshore fishing boat—its cluster of frayed black flags on long slender poles fluttering in the stern. They were used to mark the buoys but they made her look fantastical, like a funeral ship out of a Viking legend.

'That's him!' hissed Maddy urgently.

'Who? What are you talking about?'

Flora, busy searching for the Fishing Museum, didn't even turn round. She was beginning to think the place didn't exist. That her memory was playing tricks and she'd imagined that visit, years ago . . .

'Look! That man—the one that lives on board the *Raider.*'

Flora's head whipped round. 'Where?'

But you couldn't miss that shambling bulk, the shaven

head, black seaboots, grey overcoat. He was sitting on a red
fish box with his back propped against a stripped down
diesel engine. His legs were sprawled out in front of him
and he was tilting a bottle to his lips.

'He's drunk!' exclaimed Maddy with a shudder of
disgust. 'Come on, let's go. I don't like him. He gives me
the creeps—'

But even as she was talking the man lurched to his feet,
teetered dangerously close to the edge of the dock, then
staggered off, in the direction of the breaker's yard and the
Raider.

'There it is!' cried Flora. 'I could've sworn it was round
here somewhere.'

The building was much smaller than she remembered—
only single storey, squeezed between two vast, rambling
Victorian ruins that had once been the dockside offices of
rich trawler owners. But the brass plaque on the wall stated
'Maritime and Fishing Museum'. So Flora pushed open the
door.

'Where is everybody?'

There was no one at the pay desk inside the entrance. No
signs of life anywhere. Just a stark, dingy room with a semi-
circle of empty chairs round a television set. 'Educational
Video' said a hand-written notice on the wall. Beyond that
was another door. And above it was a yellow arrow and a
sign saying 'THIS WAY'.

I don't remember, Flora was thinking, it being this much
of a dump.

There were a few dreary exhibits—a model trawler in a
smeared glass case, some grey photographs and a card with
clots of rope stuck to it, 'Seamen's Knots', it said underneath. It all looked as if it hadn't been disturbed for years.

'Do you have to pay?' asked Maddy anxiously, looking
round for an adult to tell them what to do. 'We'd better go.
Maybe it's not open to the public. Maybe we shouldn't be
here at all.' She tugged Flora's sleeve. 'There's no one on
the desk, is there? It can't be open if there's no one on the
desk.'

'It's all right. They've probably gone off for a tea break or something. And it's probably free anyway. Here . . .' There was a collection box on the counter, a blue plastic model of a lifeboat. Flora slipped some coins into it. 'We've paid. OK? So let's go in.'

They ignored the video, warned off by that ring of hard classroom chairs and the description 'educational'. Instead, they followed the yellow arrow through the first door.

Inside the door Mrs Pederson was braiding a fishing net.

Maddy, in a spasm of shock, clenched Flora's arm. Her clawed hand bit so deeply that Flora squirmed out of her grip.

The woman was sitting with her back to them, hunched on a three-legged stool, threading a wooden braiding needle through a fishing net. The net hung down like a curtain. She had Mrs Pederson's grey wiry hair and her apron, sprigged with pink and blue flowers.

Maddy's face was ashen and, for one startling moment, Flora thought her legs were going to give way—she grasped Maddy's skiing jacket to hold her up. 'It's just a model,' she explained, peering into Maddy's face. 'Just a life-size model, that's all. I remember now. They used to have lots of models here, of fishermen and that.'

But Maddy didn't react. She was still staring at the net, at Mrs Pederson threading the needle through. She could almost see the net growing, before her eyes.

'Did you hear me? I said it's only a model. It doesn't even look real.'

'I heard you.'

But the haunted look was still on Maddy's face. She imagined that, every morning, when the caretaker came to unlock this room, Mrs Pederson would be frozen on her stool, like she was now, but the fishing net in her hands would have grown and grown, tumbling on to the floor and all around her like a bridal train. And beside her that bale of twine would have unwound itself and disappeared.

Then, horrified, she thought she saw the chin lift slowly, very slowly and the head begin to turn in her direction—

'It's a crap model,' laughed Flora. 'Look, it's one of those that they put in shop windows.'

Maddy shook her head, viciously, to make reality jolt back into place.

She looked again. And she could see that it wasn't Mrs Pederson's face. It was nothing like her. It was the shiny plastic face of a shop window mannequin under a silly wig.

'I thought she'd come to life,' whispered Maddy in an appalled voice. 'I must be going crazy.'

She put both hands up to her face and dragged them downwards, over her eyes and nose and mouth. But it didn't wipe away the thought of Mrs Pederson's stooped figure, in the room of nets, with her needle sliding backwards and forwards, backwards and forwards through the mesh in a dreamy, hypnotic rhythm—

'I've got to get some air.' Maddy stumbled to the door.

Outside, she sat down on the steps, her head drooping like someone dizzy and close to fainting. Tawny hair hung down in waves so her face was hidden. Her hands rested on her knees. Above the oily dock water a gang of seagulls fought like a whirling snowstorm over some titbit or other. But Maddy didn't look up. Only her fingers twitched as she picked away at a loose bit of cotton on her jeans.

Just along the coast, feathery grey smoke drifted into the sky. The man who lived aboard the *Raider* was lighting a fire on the beach, to warm his cold hands.

Flora poked around in the Fishing Museum. She didn't know what she expected to find. Lists of men lost at sea, perhaps, and the dates when they died. Or old newspaper clippings about the *Raider*'s legendary trip, in 1952, at Christmas time. But this place was as run-down and neglected as the rest of the docks. There was only one other room, with a life-size model of a seaman in oilskins hauling on a tatty piece of trawl net. He was a joke. He had the glazed moronic face of a shop window dummy and smooth pink plastic hands. Apart from him, there were various scattered objects, grimy with dust. A ship's bell, a stuffed seagull, a chart of Arctic waters . . . Flora yawned with boredom and disappointment. No luck here. The truth about Laurie's last days remained obstinately locked in history. She'd reached a dead end.

She wandered back into the first room, sat down in the front row of chairs, staring at the blank TV screen. Without thinking, she pressed the 'On' button, just for company, while she brooded on her next move.

Her listless gaze was only half aware of a bird's eye view of the fish docks, bristling with masts. 'The docks in more prosperous times,' a voice from the TV told her. Flora let her head sag and studied her boots while the commentary yakked on:

' . . . shot in December 1952 with a Super 8 cine camera by a member of the crew. This archive film takes us right on board the *Arctic Raider* on that epic, record-breaking trip.'

'What?' Flora's startled eyes jerked back to the television.

She saw a wild bucking chaos of rigging, warps and masts, a blur of spray, men in oilskins slithering among the gleaming fish. She strained her eyes, bewildered, trying to make sense of the mayhem on the screen. The picture slewed to the right to show a churning grey sea. 'Harsh conditions,' said the commentary. 'Bad weather coming.' Waves crashing over the whaleback, a fish basket skittering down deck. Then jagged scratches on the film broke up the picture—and in the next clear shot she was staring straight into Laurie's eyes.

He was crouching on the deck in sloshing water, his face haggard under a woollen hat, his blond hair wet, streaked across his forehead. He was staring straight into the camera. 'Please God somebody help me'—those burning eyes seemed to Flora to send that message personally to her across the years. She leapt up from her seat to pause the film. But there were no controls. It just ran on.

'Arctic waters,' said the voice-over. 'Christmas Day.' The violent tipping motion calmed to a soft rocking. The *Raider*, glittering with icicles, was gliding silent and serene through a gently swelling sea. 'Christmas dinner in the galley,' gushed the commentary, 'with all the crew enjoying hearty Christmas fare, just like mother makes at home.'

A dark, crowded picture, the camera roving over grinning faces, woolly sweaters, littered plates. Laurie wasn't there. 'But there's one crew member still on duty,' quipped the commentary. 'One person who won't leave his post even for Christmas dinner.'

Greedily, Flora's eyes locked on to the tracking camera as it sought out the missing crewman. Her fingernails dug purple bruises in the soft flesh of her palms. She was sure it would be Laurie. The camera's eye hovered jerkily round the ice-crusted rigging, then fixed itself on to the windows of the bridge. It lingered there. A face, for an instant only, came into focus then blurred again. It was a gaunt, hawk face. A face that Flora recognized. But even if she didn't, the commentary told her who it was.

'And there's a rare sighting of the man who made the *Raider* the queen of the fishing fleet. Known as the Iceman for his skill in Arctic waters, it's that legendary skipper, Tom Pederson.'

The film wandered off on to other topics—the fish merchants, the dockers. Flora was still staring at the screen. But she didn't see anything. All her attention twisted inwards as her mind struggled with this new and dreadful knowledge. Tom Pederson, Laurie's father, was the Iceman, the bastard skipper. And he'd been on board the *Raider* when his son was killed.

The TV voice droned on. Flora couldn't sit still. She was desperate to re-run the video and see Laurie's face again. It wasn't the chubby boy's face of the photos in the room of nets but haunted, hollow-cheeked, disfigured by a cruel welt, as if ten days on the *Raider* had made him into a different person. But, at the same time, she ached to rush outside to tell Maddy what she knew . . .

The urge to share her explosive secret got the better of her and, clattering the chairs aside, she made for the exit.

She was already bawling out, 'Maddy! Guess what—' when her eyes skimmed over the row of photographs she hadn't even glanced at on the way in. The second one stopped her in her tracks. They were just above her eye-

73

level, a mournful collection of grainy yellowing prints. Standing on tip-toe, she thrust her face closer. Flora didn't know it, but it was the same photo that Maddy had flicked past in the library book. Only this one had been cut straight from the pages of a newspaper.

15 January 1953 the newspaper was dated. And underneath the photo was this caption: 'Skipper Tom Pederson and his crew receive the fishing industry's top award, the Silver Cod Trophy, for their record-breaking Christmas trip on the deep water trawler, *Arctic Raider*.'

She studied the picture intently, her eyes searching among the cluster of men behind the Iceman. There were eight of them in their best suits and skinny ties. No Laurie, of course. He was under tons of ice at the bottom of the ocean by the time this photograph was taken. And *his* best suit ended up woven into the room of nets. But Mr Walters was there—with a young man's face and greased-down, slicked-back hair. So were other faces she recognized from the film. And tacked on the end, a little apart from the others, was the grim, stubbled face of the man in the grey overcoat. The man who lived inside the *Raider*.

Flora's breath hissed in through her teeth. 'It's you!' There was no doubt of it. Forty years had not changed him much. And he, like the Iceman, had been on board the *Raider* at the precise moment of Laurie's death.

'Why weren't you in the film?' she demanded. But the surly face glowered back at her and told her nothing. 'Hang on! I know why. You were the one shooting that film, weren't you? That's why you couldn't be in it.'

She was excited now. She was on the trail again. The true story of Laurie's death was on the point of bursting open like a rotten fruit.

Without a second thought, she grabbed the picture from the wall. It was evidence. And she wanted to show it to Maddy. Without proof, who would believe the shattering discoveries she had made in this sad, forgotten little place?

When she raced outside, the silver eagle on Maddy's jacket was glittering in the distance, by the railway line.

'Maddy! Wait a minute.' Flora panted after her. 'Maddy, I've got something to tell you. You're not going to believe it!'

Maddy turned round, resentfully, because she'd been caught sneaking off. 'What do you want? I'm going to the mall, buy some presents, some Christmas tree decorations. I've seen these glass angels—'

'But look at this.'

Maddy gave the picture a suspicious sidelong glance. 'You been nicking things again?' was her only comment.

'Look at it properly,' pleaded Flora.

'Don't shove it in my face, then.'

Maddened by impatience, Flora hung over Maddy's shoulder while she checked out the photo. 'Don't you see,' she burst out. 'That's Laurie's father, Mr Pederson. He was skipper of the *Raider* when Laurie died. So why did Laurie write that in his journal: Please God somebody help me? Why did he have to write that when his own dad was on board?'

But even as she was saying those words, Flora was very well aware that fathers don't necessarily protect you. 'And that guy on the end, look.' She stabbed her finger at the photo. 'Do you recognize him? He's the guy we saw just now, the one that lives aboard the *Raider*.'

Maddy's eyes, when she finally looked up from the picture, were deeply troubled. She couldn't speak, her emotions were too tangled. But the question she finally chose to ask seemed, in the circumstances, totally irrelevant.

'So you don't think this Laurie was a wimp, then?'

Flora stared at her. 'Are you serious?'

Maddy shrugged. 'Sorry.'

Maddy's experiences were totally different to Flora's. She sometimes rowed with her father, stormed off, sulked. But in the end, when she needed help, she was sure of getting it. The idea of Laurie, betrayed, unprotected, and, for reasons she didn't yet understand, unable to appeal to his father, moved her to pity—and anger. So, although she came at it from a different direction, her reaction to Laurie's plight on board the *Raider* turned out to be remarkably similar to Flora's. Heightened by the fact that, in the last day or so, she had had devastating personal experience of what it felt like to be alone and helpless and afraid.

'Sorry,' she said again. 'It must have been a nightmare aboard that boat.'

'I think,' said Flora, 'that we should find out what really happened on the *Raider*. I think we should find out all about that bastard skipper.' She was going to say that she thought it was their responsibility, a task that they couldn't shirk. That, somehow, Laurie was depending on them.

But she was certain Maddy would scoff at that. Even she had to admit it sounded weird.

'OK,' Maddy said.

'What?'

'I said OK, didn't I? Let's do it.'

For a moment, Flora was too stunned to reply. Maddy was full of surprises. Flora was sure that she knew Maddy's type: selfish, spoiled, attention-seeking. She would have bet anything that when she asked Maddy to join her as Laurie's champion, Maddy would reply, 'I'd rather go Christmas shopping.'

'Only I don't know,' Maddy was saying, 'why Mrs Pederson never told me about Laurie's father being skipper of the *Raider*. I mean, she must have known.'

'Perhaps she was too ashamed of what happened to Laurie,' suggested Flora.

'I don't think so. She didn't know what happened to him. According to her, Laurie loved it on board the *Raider*. She thought he was having a good time. She didn't know that anything was wrong . . .' Maddy frowned. She was pretty sure that Mrs Pederson hadn't mentioned it. But she couldn't exactly remember. After she'd dismissed Laurie as boring and immature, she'd closed her mind to what Mrs Pederson was saying about him.

'I think,' said Flora, 'that we should go and see this guy at the end of the photo. He'll know when Laurie died, won't he? He'll know what really happened.'

76

'What? Him?' Maddy thought with alarm of that sour breath, that skin like dangling pouches on his neck, that shaved skull. 'He looked crazy to me. What if he's dangerous?'

'We'll run away.'

'Oh. Right.' Maddy thought a while. 'Are you going to take that back now?' she said, eyeing the photo.

'I don't think so.' Flora had that defiant edge to her voice that Maddy was beginning to recognize. She folded her arms over her photo. 'It's evidence. I think I'll hang on to it just a little bit longer.'

10

As they walked together towards the breaker's yard, Flora's heart was racing. She was scared of course. But mainly it was excitement that made her heart thump so wildly. She felt that, at last, they were closing in on the truth.

They found the man crouching on the beach among great banks of rotting seaweed. The metal hulk of the *Raider* loomed over him. He was feeding driftwood into the flames of a small fire. As they came nearer they could hear it spit and crackle, see smoke furling up into the freezing air. The air smelt of salt and woodsmoke and rancid seaweed.

Maddy grabbed Flora's arm, hissed 'Be careful!' as if she took it for granted that Flora would make the first approach.

Flora crept closer. The man, his grey overcoat wrapped around him like a blanket, was sitting back now, among the stones and shells. She could see his face. It was the face of a hard drinker. Teeny veins webbed his nose and cheeks. His eyes were watery and rimmed with pulpy red. But they were a striking light blue, anxious and restless.

Flora's feet scrunched on the shells. Slowly, his walrus head turned to look at her and those light-blue eyes fixed on her like spotlights.

'Excuse me,' she stuttered.

She could feel Maddy, crowding behind her, feel hot breath on her neck. 'Excuse me.' In her mind she was sifting desperately through all the possible opening sentences, all the long and complex introductions she could make. But in the end she abandoned them all and just said, 'We want to know what happened to Laurie Pederson on that trip on the *Raider* in 1952.'

A bolt of surprise shot through the man's blue eyes. Then he sighed. His head sank down, exhausted, and he seemed to be staring at a spot on the beach between his boots.

But Flora had noticed things about him. She was used to watching, assessing people's moods and reactions to see if they presented any threat. And she had noticed that, although that shaven skull made him seem brutal, that stubbled baggy face, those droopy spaniel eyes, made him look self-pitying and weak. His hands hung flabbily between his knees.

'Did you hear me?' she said, risking a little severity in her voice. 'You were on the *Arctic Raider*, weren't you?'

She could feel Maddy fidgeting behind her. Maddy still thought the man was dangerous. She was repelled by those thick blue veins that crawled like slugs under the skin of his hands. The pink scalp that showed through his grizzled hair made her shiver. She was scared of ugliness, and sickness. It was obvious the man was sick. His baggy face had a grey and deathly tinge and when he spoke phlegm rattled in his throat.

'Yes,' said the man, raising his head wearily. 'I was the cook.'

He had a bottle jutting out of his overcoat pocket. But he wasn't drunk yet.

'I want to know about Laurie,' said Flora, more gently, moving closer to the fire.

'Laurie?' mumbled the cook. 'Laurie was a good boy. Born to the sea. He loved the sea. Loved it on board the *Arctic Raider*. He was a skipper in the making, that boy was.'

'Crap,' said Maddy.

The cook turned accusing eyes upon her. 'Why don't you ask his dad? Why do you have to come pestering me? It's years ago, a lifetime ago. I've forgotten all about it.'

'No, you haven't,' said Flora with sudden intuition. 'And in any case, we can't ask Mr Pederson. His wife just died yesterday.'

'Are you sure?'

Flora, usually so good at reading expressions, couldn't tell whether the cook's eyes were clouded with sorrow, or relief.

'We were there,' said Maddy bluntly, her disgust swamped by a desperate need to get this over with. To make him tell them—so this Laurie business would be off her mind and she could get on with Christmas. 'We saw the ambulance take her away.'

'So she's dead, then,' said the cook in a dazed voice. 'And what about him, the Iceman? I've heard tell he's finished, washed up. That he never goes out—just makes model boats all the time.'

'He does make model boats,' agreed Flora. 'I've seen them.'

Her cautious reply was seized on by the cook, as if it was the sign that he'd been looking for. 'It's true, then.' He shook his head, wonderingly. 'Then there's no need for me to lie any more,' he said.

'So will you tell us the truth about Laurie?'

There was a long silence while the cook considered this. Finally, he shrugged and patted the sand beside him. 'Come and sit down.'

'Er, I don't think we will,' said Maddy, nudging Flora in the ribs. 'I think we'll just stand here.'

'Sit down,' growled the cook. 'I'm not going to hurt you. I'm a sick old man.'

Warily, they eased themselves down among pebbles, making sure that the fire was between them and the cook. Maddy had wild ideas of sticking a burning brand in his face if he made a lunge at them. Her nose twitched in disgust—his overcoat stank like a wet dog.

But he didn't even look at them. He was staring trance-like into the fire's glowing depths. They thought he was dozing but he was trawling in his memories, bringing them slithering up to the surface like the *Raider*'s net rising from the sea.

He remembered Laurie all right. Laurie, a big awkward uncoordinated boy. Laurie, who was never born to the sea. Who was too dreamy, too slow to react. He should have been safe at home, reading boy's adventures in a cosy armchair. At sea he was a liability, a Jonah. It only took a couple of days to establish his incompetence, his lack of stamina and muscle power. And then the jokes got cruel. There was no pity for Laurie on the *Raider*. Someone like him could get you killed, maimed. Lose you money.

On his first day, three hours out from port, they put him in the fishroom, chopping ice. It was an important job. If the fishroom wasn't properly prepared, then all the boxes of fish would rot, the entire catch was ruined.

Laurie, arms aching, hands bleeding, was in there shovelling ice. After two hours he'd fallen asleep, leaning on the shovel.

'Eh, come 'ere!' It was that little weasel, Eddie Walters, the one that tormented Laurie most, calling out to the rest of the crew. 'Come and look at this, the useless little bugger!'

And the cook, like the rest, had gone running.

'He's asleep!' crowed Eddie, happy to catch Laurie out. 'He's ruddy well asleep!'

Crowding round the door they'd seen Eddie kick the shovel away. Watched Laurie sprawl among the glittering ice. There had been harsh appreciative laughter from the men. It served him right. On the *Raider* falling asleep at your post was a crime, like a soldier sleeping on duty. The Iceman had seen them from the bridge, heard what was going on but he hadn't interfered. After that, Laurie was fair game . . .

Maddy and Flora stayed quiet. The cook seemed to have forgotten all about them. The fire spit sparks on to his coat but he didn't notice. Just behind him, the *Raider*'s grey walls reared up, menacing as a medieval fortress.

Maddy eased her cramped leg. She was bored now, rather than afraid.

'Look,' she demanded. 'Are you going to tell us anything or not? I mean, what happened on the *Raider*. Didn't Laurie get on with the crew or something?'

The cook's mocking bark of laughter made her shrink back. But the laughter ended in a helpless coughing fit.

'Didn't get on with them!' spluttered the cook. 'I'll say he didn't get on with them! They crucified him, that's what they did! He was a Jonah, a ruddy liability. Always dreamy, falling asleep, always in the wrong place. He was too dangerous to have on deck—nobody wanted to work alongside him.'

The cook was getting worked up, his jowls quivering, his shaved head jerking in and out of his baggy neck like an old turtle. 'He couldn't crack ice, couldn't handle a gutting knife. He let it slip into one bloke's leg. He couldn't even fill the needles on time. His mind was always somewhere else. And he held up the trawl. Nobody did that on the *Raider*. Nobody ever held up the trawl.'

The cook fumbled in his pocket and lit a cigarette with shaking hands.

'But he was only just 16,' objected Maddy. 'He'd never been to sea before.' She turned to Flora, looking for support. But Flora was lost in her own thoughts.

'What's that matter?' said the cook, calmer now. 'He couldn't do the job. He was a liability, that's what mattered.'

'He was only a boy. Why didn't somebody look after him?' demanded Maddy, who took being looked after, sheltered and protected, for granted.

The cook just shrugged, as if he couldn't begin to explain the situation on the *Raider* to somebody like her. 'Being a boy didn't make no difference,' he murmured, as if that was an answer.

'So what happened to him?' asked Flora quietly. 'What did you do to him?'

'I didn't do nothing!' The cook's voice was a whine of protest. 'I tried to protect him. I saved his dinners when they said he couldn't have none. I gave him extra custard. He loved custard. But he was his own worst enemy. And the crew took against him—they was on to him all the time. Putting shackles in his bunk so he couldn't sleep. Making him scrub the deck with a toothbrush when big seas were coming in. Nobody liked him, except me. They said he was a Jonah. They said he was the reason we weren't catching any fish—'

'What stupid superstition!' interrupted Maddy.

The cook shrugged again. Impossible to explain to them the atmosphere on the *Raider*. Going on to the fishing ground was like going into battle. The Iceman up in his glass cage—there was nothing escaped his eye. If there was a single tear in the trawl net, he'd see it. He never slept, hardly ate, on the fishing grounds. Just lived on adrenalin. Pacing the bridge like it was a war room, bawling orders, absolutely in control, driving the men until they were near crazy with fatigue.

Flora, her voice tense and anguished, asked the question that for her probed to the heart of Laurie's story. 'Why didn't his dad protect him? He must have known what was going on.'

'The Iceman knew everything that was going on.'

'Then why didn't he stop the bullying?'

'Bullying?' The cook gave a brief bitter laugh at the use of that playground word. He tipped the ash off his cigarette into the flames.

'I'll tell you, shall I? I'll tell you about the Iceman. He was cold as ice, no feelings—that's how he really got his name. He was a gentleman on shore. Kind to dogs and old ladies. But at sea he wasn't even human. Specially when the fishing started. He wanted to make a name for himself, see, to make more money than any other skipper. He was crazy. He never ran for shelter while there was good fishing left. He broke every safety rule in the book. Nothing would make him stop fishing, not even God Almighty. He'd fish in the black dark with seas coming over washing men out of the pounds and he'd be screaming from the bridge like a madman, "Shoot the trawl. Shoot it away!" He was crazy, a beast when he was fishing, not human. He didn't eat, didn't sleep until the gear was stowed . . . crazy . . .'

Hands still trembling, the cook took a hungry drag on his cigarette. He could see the incomprehension on their faces. But then one of them made a comment which seemed to show some spark of understanding.

'So you're saying,' said Flora, 'that the Iceman knew about what was happening to his son? How the crew were making his life hell. But that he didn't stop it. That he even approved of it?'

The cook looked sharply at her. But she'd lowered her eyes again. 'He approved of it all right. He wanted the crew to toughen him up. He was ashamed of Laurie being so soft. He thought his mother had brought him up too soft. Thought he should be toughened up a bit. He thought it was for the boy's own good.'

'How could he do that?' cried Maddy. 'How could his own father just stand by and let that happen to him?'

Flora said nothing.

'And you said you liked him!' raged Maddy. 'Why didn't you do something?'

'I tried,' mumbled the cook. 'I did what I could.'

But for forty years his conscience had been troubled, now and again, about Laurie. About whether he should have done more. But it wasn't easy. As a cook his own standing with the crew was precarious. They had a deep contempt for all the 'down-below' men, those like him, who had 'soft' jobs that didn't risk life and limb every time the trawl net was shot and hauled. So he couldn't afford to get on the wrong side of them. It was more than his job was worth to protect Laurie. He'd done what he could.

When they wouldn't let Laurie down to the galley for his dinner, the cook had saved his helping of apple pie and custard in one of those big, empty corned beef cans. He'd watched the boy, streaming with water, shivering so much that the spoon clattered on his teeth, wolfing it down. Looking over his shoulder in case Eddie Walters or some other member of the crew came down and caught him.

In those first few days, Laurie crept, whenever he could, into the warmth of the galley. The cook had never been shown so much respect. The poor little sod was excessively polite. Even called him 'sir' as if he was a schoolmaster.

'Oh yes, sir, I love fishing. She's a smashing ship isn't she, sir, the *Raider*. Best I've ever been on.' And all the time his hands would be shaking round his mug of tea and he'd be looking round at the galley door with wide fearful eyes.

The cook was very well aware that the boy saw him as his only friend, thought he might protect him. But in the end, even the cook had driven him out of his one warm refuge: 'They'll have my hide if they find you in here again!'

'He was a nice, polite boy, was Laurie,' said the cook, wiping his eyes with the cuff of his rough coat.

'When did he die?' asked Flora softly.

'What do you mean?' said the cook with a last, juicy sniff.

'His mother said he died in January, after the trip was over and the *Raider* was only a day away from home. But he didn't, did he? He died on Christmas Day. Why did you all lie about when he died?'

The cook shuffled on the sand. He squinted up at the hazy winter sun. 'The pubs will be open soon,' he said.

'I just want you to tell me that, that's all.'

'I suppose,' said the cook, 'it don't matter now she's dead.'

When the fishing stopped and the madness ended and the *Raider* was steaming home with the fishroom full to bursting, they'd sent a radio message back to shore about Laurie's death. But not until January 3rd. And then, in a conspiracy of shame and guilt, they had to keep up with the lie. And other lies. His mother thought he was a hero, that he played his part in winning that trophy. In fact, they'd never let him near the trawl. And he was two days' dead when they started netting record hauls.

'He went overboard,' said the cook, 'on Christmas Day.'

'Did somebody push him?' asked Flora.

'No, no,' protested the cook, shocked. But he looked at her with a sly respect. 'Nobody did that. It was an accident. He was the only one on deck. We were all down the galley having Christmas dinner. The Iceman was up on the bridge. You saw the film, didn't you? I saw you going into the Fishing Museum. Did you see my film?'

Flora nodded, silently.

'I was interested in cameras then. I used to film a bit, just mess about . . .'

85

Flora nodded again, scared to speak in case she broke the thread of his memories.

'Well, Laurie was on his own on the deck, filling needles. They said he couldn't have his Christmas dinner until he was finished. It was a long time before anybody noticed he hadn't come down. I sent someone up on deck, see, to call him down for his dinner. But he was gone, and the basket of needles with him. Just washed over the side.'

'Didn't you go back and search for him?' asked Maddy, appalled.

The cook sighed. 'It wouldn't have been no good. The *Raider* was under full steam. By the time the Iceman eased her down, turned her round . . . and it was getting dark. Two, three minutes, that's all he would last in a sea like that. He didn't have a cat in hell's chance.' The cook added, 'It wouldn't 'ave been no use.'

'Then why didn't you radio back? Why did the Iceman carry on, after his own son was dead?'

'I've told you,' said the cook petulantly, 'what he was like. He stood to make or lose his reputation on that trip. He had a bet on with other skippers. If he'd have broke radio silence then he'd have given away his position, they'd all have known where he was fishing. And the company might have told him to come home, might have thought he wasn't fit to carry on. And he didn't want that. Not the Iceman.'

'I think that's terrible,' said Maddy. 'That his own father didn't turn back to search.'

'What was the use?' The cook sounded peeved at her lack of understanding. 'I've said—he was dead three minutes after he hit the water. We didn't even find out he was gone until maybe twenty, even thirty, minutes after.'

What he didn't say was that, in his heart, he had wanted to turn the *Raider* round to search for Laurie's body, even though he knew it was a hopeless task. It would have been a gesture, anyway. But the Iceman was like God. You didn't question his decisions. And none of the crew had wanted it. They were glad to be rid of him. They didn't want his body on board, jinxing the boat. When they found out he'd gone missing, Eddie Walters had said, 'Is that his Christmas dinner you've been saving? Pity to waste it. Give it here. He won't be coming back for it.'

'Bloody good job,' someone else had added.

And the *Raider* had gone steaming on into the history books. Probably the most famous deep water trawler of all time, with Tom Pederson the most famous skipper.

'He was what they call a Don Skipper after that trip,' the cook rambled on. 'Like a Godfather. They even made up songs about him. Everyone wanted to sail with him. He was hard but you made money. You made a fortune with the Iceman—'

'He was a bastard,' said Maddy forcefully.

The cook sighed and drew his overcoat tightly round him, to keep out the cold.

'We're going now,' said Maddy. 'Come on, Flora.' She'd had enough of him. The nasty truth was out now, like a boil burst. The mystery cleared up—the Laurie business over.

Flora got up obediently.

But as Maddy strode away, Flora turned to the cook and their eyes met for a moment in a look of helpless sorrow. She should have hated him, for being weak, for failing to protect Laurie. But she couldn't blame him. He'd done what he could.

She turned away and followed Maddy.

The cook watched them go. The fire had gone out and he felt cold and ill, exhausted by these old painful memories. He didn't think he would go to the pub tonight. He hoisted himself up and floundered out over the mud, weaving through the twisted bits of metal. The gangplank bulged under his weight. Then he crept into the darkness inside the *Arctic Raider*. 'He was a Godfather, though,' he was murmuring to himself. 'A Don Skipper. The best there ever was.'

Back on the beach, by the pile of charred driftwood, lay the photo of the Iceman and his crew. Flora had forgotten to take it with her. The tide surged in around the silent wreck

of the *Raider* and tiptoed up the beach. It foamed around
the photo. Then lifted it up. The image of the best skipper
there ever was receiving his Silver Cod Trophy, swirled out
on the ebb tide, to be lost in the open sea.

11

When they reached the disused railway line, Maddy turned to Flora and announced, 'That's that, then. Thank God it's all over.' The shopping mall beckoned. 'Listen!' she urged Flora. 'You can hear a brass band, playing carols.'

She wanted to forget Laurie's bizarre and tragic story, flush the harrowing details from her mind. She wanted to think about happy things. But the experiences of the past two days had disturbed her more than she cared to admit. They had given her complacent little world a savage shaking. And try as she might, the pieces wouldn't fit back together as smoothly as before.

Flora confirmed her worst fears. 'It's not over yet,' she said. 'We haven't talked to Mr Pederson yet.'

'For Christ's sake,' protested Maddy. 'Don't you ever give up?' Her dismay made her sound aggressive. She was scared of that defiant look on Flora's face. She wanted to forget about the Pedersons. If there were any more stones left to turn over, any more horrors writhing underneath, she didn't want to know about them.

'Let's just drop it, shall we?' she pleaded with Flora. 'We've gone as far as we can go. We found out when he died and everything. I mean, there's no mystery now, is there? I hate what happened to Laurie just as much as you. But it was ages ago. It's ancient history. Who cares about it now?'

'I care.' Flora beat at her own chest to emphasize the point in a gesture so violent, so unFlora-like, that Maddy had to stop herself giggling in alarm. 'I care,' repeated Flora, her face grim and obstinate. 'And I've got to go and see the Iceman. I've got some questions to ask him.'

'I think it's a crazy idea. Don't you know when to stop? I mean, what questions are you going to ask him? What else is there to know?'

'I'm not sure yet.'

Maddy raised her eyes to heaven and sighed. 'Well, do what you like. But you'll have to go on your own. I'm sick to death of the whole business. I'm not going to let it spoil *my* Christmas.'

She flounced off across the road, glaring at a driver who had to stomp on his brakes to avoid mowing her down.

Flora gazed after her. She would rather have had Maddy with her. She'd got used to her company—she felt scared of doing this alone. But she mustn't think about that. She closed down her mind, put on her stone face in case fear or self-doubt should distract her from her purpose.

Then she hunched her shoulders, dug her cold, tingling hands into her pockets and started walking.

Flora slid out of the dark bushes that crowded up to the Iceman's workshop. He was in there all right, surrounded by his plans and tools and tiny tins of paint, all arranged with obsessive neatness. But she shouldn't have hesitated— she should have marched straight in. For when she saw him, when she had a good, close look at him, she could find no connection with the screaming tyrant that the cook had talked about. She hardly knew what she expected—a cruel hawk face perhaps, a predator's face with manic eyes. But he seemed quite distinguished, gentlemanly, with a long bony face and a mane of grey hair. He had been tall once, but he was stooped now and shrunken. There was nothing menacing about him.

He was carving yet another fragile model ship. Yet as she saw how gently he shaved off the wood, how lovingly he turned the *Raider* over and over in his hands, she felt a familiar anger boiling like acid inside her. Laurie's misery and her own became mixed up in her mind. How dare he lavish so much tender attention on a block of wood when he'd neglected his own son so ruthlessly? She thought of Laurie, condemned to cruel treatment and misery and self-contempt, when all the time his own father had been

90

watching what was happening from his glass cage. Her mind flashed up an image of her own father, watching from a window, yet pretending not to see.

Rage, pity for Laurie, pity for herself, swelled in her throat until she thought it would burst and choke her. She had come here as Laurie's champion but when she stormed into the Iceman's lair, it was for herself, just as much as Laurie, that she was going into battle. Her mind was hyperactive, whirling, gobbling like a turkey. She didn't have a rational thought in her head. But she carried into that workshop, like a flaming torch, a burning sense of a high-noon confrontation with all the forces that oppressed her— the bullies, those who sanctioned them, her own crippling fear and self-doubt. No more running, no more hiding, no more stone faces. Time for a showdown.

None of her class-mates would have known her now. She barely knew herself. They all thought her passive, gentle, unresisting. Easy to ignore. No one, except perhaps Maddy, had any idea of the violent resentment locked up deep inside.

The Iceman jerked his head up, dazed, as this avenging fury gate-crashed his private workshop. Even the late Mrs Pederson hadn't been allowed in here.

'You knew,' Flora hissed at him, bitter bile almost choking her. 'You knew what was happening to Laurie on board the *Arctic Raider*, didn't you?'

She wanted the impact of her question to be mortal. She wanted it to strike him as a harpoon strikes a whale, exploding in its guts.

But he hardly reacted at all. Just stared at her, vaguely, as if she was a minor distraction to his model making.

She moved in closer, spitting out venomous accusations. 'You were ashamed of Laurie, weren't you? You thought he was soft, that he needed toughening up. You didn't protect him at all, did you? Even though you knew what was going on. You didn't lift a finger to help him, did you?'

She felt terribly close to losing self-control. All her life, she had practised self-control, put on a stone face, carried on relentlessly, pretending her way of life was normal. She had never known such rage as she felt now, as if she was spinning towards self-destruction and there'd be nothing left of her but blue smoke and a pile of ashes. And when the Iceman looked at her like that—in that half-mocking, dismissive kind of way as if she was insignificant—

'Answer my question,' she yelled at him, distraught. 'Don't you dare turn away like that! I'm asking you about your son, Laurie, your only son. So you answer my question!'

To her horror, his eyes actually slid from her face back to the model he was making. He even picked it up. She couldn't believe what she was seeing. She wanted to smash the flimsy wooden model from his hands and watch it splinter on the floor.

But at last he spoke to her.

His voice seemed calm and unconcerned. 'You're that girl, aren't you? The one that came round to see me about fishing but saw my wife instead? Well, you know then, don't you. You know how Laurie loved the sea. How he was born to the sea. My wife must have told you.'

'I'm not that girl. That was another girl. But I've been talking to her. And I've been talking to the cook.'

'Ah. He's still alive, is he? Well, let me tell you something—you shouldn't believe everything the cook tells you.'

He'd been varnishing something: the sickly smell tickled in Flora's nostrils. He took up his wood-carving knife as if he was cutting himself off from her.

She wanted to reach out and shake him violently. Really hurt him. Nothing she said seemed to get through to him. His eyes were detached as if his mind was far away, still sailing distant oceans.

Flora would almost have welcomed the shrieking maniac the cook had described. She just didn't know how to deal with this total lack of emotion.

'Who killed Laurie?' Her voice was so strangled with fury that she could hardly force the words out. She hadn't meant to ask this question. She'd accepted the cook's explanation of Laurie's death as an accident. 'Did somebody push him? Did you push him?' She wanted her outrageous question to drag him, kicking and screaming, from whatever far ocean his mind was sailing on. She wanted to blast through that remoteness, that self-contained disinterest that seemed to say, 'Laurie? What's his death got to do with me?'

She was beginning to feel unreal—that familiar feeling, as if she was a shadow girl, ghostly and insubstantial. She tried to get a grip on herself, breathing deeply, smelling the varnish, feeling the rough wood of the workbench where she'd slammed her fists down.

When he answered her question with an abstracted half-smile she could have killed him. 'I don't know where you've got all this information from, young lady,' he said. 'But it's completely wrong, you know. Laurie's death was an accident. I saw everything that happened from the bridge . . .'

She thought, with a twist of agony deep in her stomach, that he was going to stop there. That he was going to deny her his eye-witness account of what happened. He took his time curling a woodshaving off the hull of the *Raider* before he carried on. His description of the incident was brisk, businesslike. But he kept his head bowed.

'It was a tragic accident. But not unusual. Hundreds of men were lost overboard off trawlers. Laurie was filling needles and a wave washed the basket overboard. He tried to grab it and went over the rail. I thought he was coming back on the next wave. I was certain of it. His hands were on the rail, the ship was pulling him up . . . But then he let go and disappeared. And it was too late. We were steaming full ahead, it was getting dark and the sea was freezing up. By the time I'd eased down, turned her round,' he shrugged and shook his head, 'there was nothing I could do.'

Flora should have leapt in now with all sorts of angry protests: 'Why didn't you search for his body? Why did you lie about when he died?' But she didn't ask those questions.

93

Instead she said, in an awed and thoughtful voice, 'Did you say that he *let go* of the rail?'

'I said he lost his grip.' As he answered, the Iceman shot a sharp, suspicious look at her. He was getting flustered.

But Flora didn't notice. All her rage had left her in a sudden gush, making her weak and shivery as a new-born creature. She had just had a revelation. It thudded like a spear into her mind then opened like the bloom of a brilliant flower.

'Don't you see?' she appealed in desperation to the Iceman. 'Don't you see what Laurie did? He could have saved himself. But he didn't. He believed what everyone was saying about him. He believed that he was no good, useless, that he was ruining your chances of the trophy. So he let go for you.'

Flora spoke with scorching conviction. She was absolutely sure, from her own experiences, that she knew what was going through Laurie's mind when he made that last dreadful choice.

'He thought he was bad luck, a Jonah like everybody said. He thought he didn't deserve to go on living. So he let go. He hated himself, see. He believed he was a coward. And he knew you were up there, watching. So he did it for you. He knew you were ashamed of him. He was trying to make you proud of him. Don't you understand that?'

The Iceman didn't crumble, as she'd hoped he would. How could he look so unmoved when she herself was gulping back tears? He was impregnable, like a high fortified castle. She could pound on the walls, lay siege to the door but she wouldn't even leave a dent.

She gave up, defeated, wrung dry by the new and unbearable knowledge of Laurie's wasted sacrifice.

Unbelievably, the Iceman had opened up a pot of paint.

I hate you, you cold bastard, she decided with startling clarity. I know how you operate. I know how people like you operate. You made Laurie think that he didn't exist unless he got your approval, unless you were proud of him. But you never were, were you? You never were.

She didn't say this to him. She just assumed it wasn't worth it. She turned round and went out, leaving him on his own, in his workshop.

'Let's forget him, Laurie,' she found herself murmuring. 'He's not worth bothering with. He's washed up, finished, like the cook said. People like him aren't worth bothering with.'

It was a healing, liberating thought—one that she had never dared think before. 'People like him aren't worth bothering with,' she said again. 'We don't need them, do we?'

She almost bumped into Maddy, waiting for her by the front gate. 'Where'd you come from?'

'Oh,' shrugged Maddy, 'just decided I'd better come over. See what you were up to, make sure you didn't get into any trouble.'

She felt a fool, now that she was here. It had been warm and friendly in the shopping mall, cosy with Christmas cheer. She'd just bought a Christmas star for her bedroom. She was moving in on the wrapping paper—when suddenly she'd stopped dead in the middle of the aisle. People had bumped into her. 'Oh God!' she'd groaned. 'I suppose I'd better see if she's all right.' And she'd stalked off, towards the exit.

'You needn't have come,' said Flora. 'Nothing happened.'

'I know I *needn't* have come,' said Maddy, dangerously, through gritted teeth. 'But I'm here now. OK?'

Flora grinned. 'Thanks.'

'Oh, Gawd,' muttered Maddy, embarrassed. 'You don't fancy a McDonald's, do you?'

'So did you say nothing happened?' asked Maddy as they waited in the queue for a table.

There were some people here who knew her. The sight of her, in Flora's company, made their jaws sag. She was surprised how little she cared.

She turned again to Flora. 'Didn't you see the Iceman, then?'

'I saw him all right,' Flora told her. 'But I might as well not have bothered. It was just a waste of breath talking to him. Nothing gets through to that man. Nothing at all.'

12

Much later that night Tom Pederson, once the most famous skipper who ever worked the northern trawl, pushed aside his model of the *Arctic Raider*. He'd been back into the house, roaming round. He'd been up to the room of nets. But he couldn't settle—so he'd come down again to his workshop.

It was dark outside but with a clear indigo sky, crowded with stars. And dead quiet—except if you listened carefully you could hear the occasional car go past along the road.

He'd come to a decision. Once, looking down from his glass cage, he'd made decisions every hour, every minute, risking men's lives. Whether to stow the gear and run for shelter, whether to take her in for repairs or whether to keep on fishing. Almost always, and sometimes against all the odds, he'd chosen to keep on fishing. And he'd been right, almost all the time. He'd been practically infallible. They said he had the luck of the devil.

He'd just made another life or death decision.

Methodical as always, he tidied away his model-making knives in gleaming rows. Then he picked up Laurie's photo. He'd brought it down from the room of nets. It was the one where the *Raider* was in her prime—and Laurie's face, proud and eager, was looking out from the top right hand corner. He brushed the dust off the glass, studied the photo for a while, then put it away, on a shelf.

He took out his cigarette lighter and applied the flame to the model *Raider* he'd been making. It was seconds before it took.

For a while, Tom Pederson watched her burn, twin flames reflected in his eyes. Then, calmly, as if he was pushing a boat across a pond on Sunday afternoon, he slid her towards the shelves at the back of the bench. It was here that he kept his bulk supplies of paint and varnish and white spirit.

Tiny flames licked along in her wake as if the *Raider* was ploughing through a burning sea. There was a moment of intense silence. Not even a car went past in the road.

From the deep shadows of the garden the workshop windows began throbbing in the dark. Then, with a livid flash that split the night sky, the whole place bloomed into a fiery orange flower.

The fireball scattered burning debris on the roof of the house and that, too, began to burn. By the time the firemen arrived, there was nothing left of the workshop or the room of nets.

The Laurie business was finished.

13

Flora's stomach clenched sharply. The pain made her wince. She felt too sick to eat breakfast. Only ten minutes ago she'd washed and put on a clean fresh blouse but already it felt hot and sticky under the arms. It was the first day back at school after the Christmas holidays. And she had all the usual boring symptoms—that familiar sweaty dread of what lay in store. Her duvet was twisted into a corkscrew. She'd thrashed around in it last night, unable to sleep. And there were bruises, deep purple like blackberry stains, under her eyes. Sighing, she patted the puffy skin tenderly. She looked a wreck.

She checked to make sure she'd got her history project, knowing that she'd checked twice before. It was a half-hearted effort, dry as old twigs. She and Maddy had just copied a few pages out of library books. There was nothing in it about Laurie or the Iceman or the room of nets or the *Raider*.

Flora was hunched on the edge of her bed, dressed in uniform, coat and gloves, school bag packed, clockwatching. She was waiting for 8.30 to click up on her radio-alarm. At 8.30 it would be time to go. Downstairs there was mayhem—doors crashing, little children squawking, 'I'll tell Mum!' Her mother's shrill voice quavering above the din, 'David, will you please stand still for just one second!' Flora hardly noticed. It was just the normal beginning to a school day.

'Flora! Flora! Are you ready yet? It's time to go!' That was her mother, shrieking up the stairs.

But it was only 8.28. Flora licked her dry lips. Two minutes left before she had to quit the snug cocoon of her bedroom and brave the world outside.

Laurie's journal was on her bedside table. It still moved her to pity when she read it—that first puppyish eagerness, that last stricken cry for help. What had happened to him still appalled her. But thinking about him didn't jangle her emotions as it used to. She felt calmer now about him, more clear-headed, as if things had been resolved. Laurie could rest in peace now. There was nothing more she could do for him.

She and Maddy had read about the fire. It had only been worth a mention in the local press. 'Ex-Skipper Dies in Fire' the headline said. The newspaper reported it as a 'tragic accident'.

'Serve him right, the cruel bastard,' said Maddy.

But Flora had kept silent, wondering. It surprised her that such a methodical man could be so careless . . .

8.30. She couldn't put it off any longer. She clasped her stomach to stop it turning somersaults. 'Stop it!' she snapped at herself. 'Grow up. Don't be such a baby.'

The last thing she put on before she left the house was that old stone face. It was her only defence against the day ahead. *They* came back rested and refreshed after the holidays, eager to sharpen up their malice on her. The first day back was always a nightmare.

Somehow she'd thought that, after Laurie, it might be different on the first day back. But, so far, things were working out just the same. The same boring rituals controlled her, the same dragging reluctance to step out on the streets.

She had no illusions about Maddy though. She wouldn't be surprised if, once she got back with her mates, Maddy didn't even acknowledge her, let alone stay friendly with her. It might not be like that. Maddy might be tough enough to shrug off the snide remarks of her friends. But Flora didn't get her hopes up. In her experience it was a bad idea, expecting too much of people.

Flora walked quickly, her head down, inspecting the cracks in the pavement. She was just about to dodge down her usual alley—the first of a network of alleyways and backstreets that bypassed Moravian Street—when she was stopped dead by a sudden resistance inside her mind.

'Laurie,' she declared out loud, 'this is crazy, isn't it? This is getting really boring.' She felt her stone face scrunch into a defiant scowl. I don't need any of this, she was thinking. Being scared, running round alleyways. I can't do this for the rest of my life, can I, Laurie?

'No, you can't,' she imagined Laurie saying, even though she knew quite well he'd been dead for forty years.

'OK, then,' agreed Flora. But like a diver, dithering with her toes curled round the top diving board, she couldn't make that plunge.

'Right,' she whispered. 'I'm going now. I'm really going now.'

She rocked forwards, back on to her heels, forwards again . . . Then with a desperate rush Flora launched herself into Moravian Street.

She forced those wobbling legs to walk slowly, forced herself to hold her head high. And all the time she was thinking of Laurie to give herself strength. She thought of how petty her own problems were compared to Laurie's suffering on the *Raider*. But, somehow, that didn't make things any easier . . . An iron gate clanged. Flora's whole body flinched. There they were, wearing uniform and sullen Monday morning faces, setting out for school.

I'm dead now, thought Flora, with weary resignation.

She felt herself tense for the first jeering remark, the first gob of spit, the first crashing collision that would send her spinning into the gutter. That always amused them. They loved to walk by casually, then, at the last moment, swerve to slam her into the nearest wall, or crowd her off the pavement. 'Whoops, sorry,' they sometimes said, choking on giggles.

They'd seen her.

Here we go, thought Flora. The same dreary, nerve-racking routine beginning all over again. You'd think they'd get tired of harassing her. But they never, ever, did . . .

Nothing happened.

They threw shifty looks in her direction. Then just walked off and left her. As if she had her own personal defence shield glowing all around her.

101

Flora gazed open-mouthed after them. For a while, she thought it was another spiteful ruse—to trick her into thinking she was safe while they waited, in some hiding place, to ambush her. But they did nothing suspicious. Just walked straight on, out of Moravian Street and across the road. She could see them quite clearly. A woman brushed by, herding a bunch of toddling kids to playschool. They lurched round Flora's legs and gawped up at her. Flora moved on. But she was walking in a daze.

She couldn't explain it. It must have been because Maddy had scared them off. But she also had a vague sense of something different in herself. As if she might be sending out new signals—signals that warned them she was stronger now, less vulnerable, more self-assured. That warned them that their hold on her was weakening.

'Come on,' Flora mocked herself, as she saw them muttering to each other. 'You're just dreaming. They don't give up that easy. They're probably just deciding what name to call you first.'

But despite her doubts, she felt exhilaration fluttering inside her.

Flora shadowed them, at a distance. She watched their feet, matching her pace to theirs with elaborate caution so the gap between them didn't narrow. If they slowed down, so did she. At any moment, she expected them to turn and confront her. But they kept walking. And they didn't once look back.

'Bitch!'

Flora almost dived into the nearest alley.

Until she realized they were shrieking at each other, not at her.

'Stupid bleeding cow!'

They were preying on each other. Standing in the middle of the pavement, screaming insults. As if bullying Flora was the only thing that united them. And now they'd lost their victim, there was nowhere else to use up all that malice—but on each other. It was a spectacular bust-up, of the hair-pulling, screeching, scratching, shin-kicking variety.

102

Flora watched, fascinated, as one of them clawed the school bag off the other's shoulders and scattered its contents in the road. They had done that to her, loads of times.

Flora gave a low, incredulous whistle. 'Amazing.' She found it unbelievable. She'd got into the habit of thinking things could never change—that skulking around backstreets and being scared was the only way to live.

Yet now she walked straight past them as they scuffled on the pavement. And felt only a tremor of unease.

A voice inside her head wittered on—telling Flora that it couldn't last, that they'd be best buddies again tomorrow. But that nagging voice couldn't stop a strange new sensation bubbling up inside her like a spring. It made her delirious, lightheaded. And at first, she didn't recognize it at all. It took her minutes to work out that this was what it felt like not to be afraid. Fear had crushed her for so long that she'd entirely forgotten what it felt like to be free.

She allowed herself a tight, cautious little smile. But inside her mind she was turning joyous cartwheels. She wanted to dance. She wanted to punch the air and yell, 'Yay! Magic!' But she just shouldered her school bag more securely and walked on.

Behind her she was aware of a pattering rush of feet, then panting, then scalding breath right on her neck. Her stomach cramped in anguish as she whirled round. It was one of her tormentors—not the ex-friend but the other one whom everyone called Carrot. Not because of her crinkly red hair but because she had teeth like a rabbit.

'Just trying to catch up with you,' gasped Carrot, falling into step beside Flora.

Flora could only stare at her. 'What do *you* want?'

'Nothing,' mumbled Carrot, sucking anxiously on her big teeth and glancing over her shoulder. 'Just thought I'd walk to school with you, that's all.'

'What?' Flora shrank back in revulsion.

'I never meant to do it,' protested Carrot. 'Call you names and that. I liked you really. It was her, her that made me do it! I never wanted to. I told her not to. But she never listened . . . And anyway it was just a joke. I didn't mean it . . . it was just a joke, that's all.'

Flora gazed, speechless, at the frantic figure tugging at her sleeve. Suddenly she wanted to hit her, smash her face in. She wanted to get her own back. But she didn't do it. She just shook her off and stalked away, leaving Carrot wailing, 'Just a joke, that's all. Just a bit of fun . . .'

For a moment Flora's emotion—grief and hurt at years of cruelty so casually dismissed by Carrot—almost broke her heart.

But then, to her own astonishment, she began to laugh at the ludicrous situation she was in. She was giggling, holding on to a garden wall for support. 'Who'd ever have believed it, Laurie? Carrot asking me to protect her. Carrot wanting to be my best friend.' She had to wipe the tears from her face with her sleeve.

'Come on,' she told herself. 'Get a move on. Stop messing about. You'll be late for school.'

There was no sign of Carrot. Carrot had slipped like a ghost down an alley. She was climbing a fence now, racing across the playing field so she could sneak into school by the back way. Flora had done that loads of times.

But today she was going in by the main gate.

Calmer now, Flora crossed the road. Buses were grinding in and out of the bus park. Students milled about.

'I don't think,' remarked Flora to Laurie, 'that after what's just happened, anything will surprise me ever again.'

But she was wrong.

For at that precise moment she caught sight of Maddy, standing by the school gates, waiting for her.

Other Oxford Fiction

It's My Life
Michael Harrison
ISBN 0 19 275042 9

As soon as he opens his front door, Martin feels that something's wrong. But he never expects the hand over his mouth, the rope around his wrists, and the mysterious man who's after a large ransom. Before Martin knows it, he's a pawn in a dangerous game that becomes more and more terrifying with every turn . . .

A Haunted Year
Ann Phillips
ISBN 0 19 275046 1

Florence is bored. The Easter holidays are dragging on—until she finds a way to summon up a ghost.

Now she has a friend to play with. George always comes when she calls him. And soon she doesn't even need to call him. And then—he won't go away . . .

No matter what Florence does or where she goes, George is always there!

Against the Day
Michael Cronin
ISBN 0 19 275039 9

It is 1940. The Nazis have invaded, and Britain is now part of the Third Reich. All over the country, German military authorities are taking control, led by the brutal Gestapo.

But slowly, surely, a resistance is building throughout the land. A secret network of people are plotting to overthrow the Nazis and win back their freedom, at any cost. Frank and Les, two schoolboys, never meant to get involved—but find themselves part of a dangerous undercover operation that can only end in bloodshed . . .

Chartbreak
Gillian Cross
ISBN 0 19 275043 7

When Janis Finch storms out of a family row, it starts a chain of events which transforms her whole life. For it's in the motorway café, minutes later, that she meets the unknown rock band, Kelp, who talk her into coming to their gig that night.

Janis goes along for the ride, and finds herself increasingly provoked by Christie, Kelp's arrogant lead singer. He pushes her into singing with them, and winds her up into a fever of rage, awe, and attraction. So when Christie asks her to join the band, Janis feels powerless to refuse—and her life explodes.

Chandra
Frances Mary Hendry
ISBN 0 19 275058 5
Winner of the Writer's Guild Award and the Lancashire Book Award

Chandra can't believe her luck. The boy her parents have chosen for her to marry seems to be modern and open-minded. She's sure they will have a wonderful life together. So once they are married she travels out to the desert to live with him and his family—only when she gets there, things are not as she imagined.

Alone in her darkened room she tries to keep her strength and her identity. She is Chandra and she won't let it be forgotten.

The House of Rats
Stephen Elboz
ISBN 0 19 275021 6
Winner of the Smarties Young Judges Prize

The great house has become a dangerous place since the master mysteriously vanished. Wolves prowl around in the snow outside, hungry and howling, while inside the house, the horrible Aphid Dunn has taken charge. Everything seems to be falling apart.

Esther and the boys are wondering if things can get any worse, when they discover a whole new world under the house. There might still be one last chance at freedom after all . . .